Buttmen

Erotic Stories and True Confessions
by Gay Men Who Love Booty

Edited by Alan Bell

WEST BEACH BOOKS

Buttmen is a West Beach Book

West Beach Books
PO Box 68406
Indianapolis, IN 46268
www.westbeachbooks.com
www.buttmenfunzone.com

Designed by Alan Bell

First Paperback Edition: July 2001
First Paperback Edition ISBN 0-9665333-0-5
ISBN may vary on electronic and eBook editions.
Preassigned LCCN: 2001090142

Buttplay for Buttmen!

✔ Vote for your favorite
   celebrity asses.

✔ Get links to hot ass sites.

✔ Read the wacky things
   Buttmen say on the net.

✔ Find out more about the
   Buttmen series.

www.buttmenfunzone.com

A great ass site
from the people who bring you
a great ass book

Buttmen

Erotic Stories and True Confessions
by Gay Men Who Love Booty

Table of Contents

A Note About Safer Sex

Buttmen: Erotic Stories and True Confessions by Gay Men Who Love Booty bears witness to various aspects of men's sexuality as it relates to the male ass. This anthology strives to provide insight into our fantasies and realities by allowing the authors to communicate freely about what they think about and what they do to explore their love of men, ass and sex.

West Beach Books acknowledges that some of the sexual acts within these pages fall outside the current definitions of safer sex. Our intent is not to condone, condemn or judge individuals or individual choice, but rather to present a forum for free expression of sexuality and sexual matters.

We do, however, encourage all Buttmen to educate themselves in all matters of sexual health, to know current medical positions on safer sex, and to take personal responsibility for one's actions with full knowledge and awareness of the potential consequences of those actions.

He crouches
next to the
boy on the

bed and draws
the edge of
his hand down

between the
buttocks with
the pleasing

smoothness of
a swipe-card
in its groove.

Gregory Woods

Rimming Krzysztof

Simon Sheppard

I like to stick my tongue up guys' assholes. I think that if we fags are honest with ourselves, many of us do. Like it, that is. Just why we like it is an open question. It is not, however, an open question as to why I hardly ever do it anymore. It comes down to a killer case of bacterial dysentery I picked up in a steamroom at the baths one misty evening many years ago. Since then I don't eat ass very often. It has nothing to do with morality or aesthetics; it's just a practical decision. I remember how lousy I felt waking up in the middle of the night with chills and cramps, and I'd rather not feel that sick again.

Now, about Krzysztof. I met him at a so-so bar one Tuesday night. We decided to go back to his place. Krzystof had come from Poland and still had a nice accent. He had that fine-boned look some Polish guys have and light blond hair that, unstylishly, touched his shoulders.

"Nice car," he said as he climbed into my Jaguar.

"I bought it used."

"It's still nice," he said. I looked over at him. Now that we were outside the bar, he looked a little shabby around the edges.

"You sure going over to your place is a good idea?"

"Sure. I have a roommate, but he won't mind."

When we got to his apartment building—in a marginal part of town that left me worried about parking the Jag—his roommate was awake, padding around in a T-shirt and boxer shorts. He was good-looking, but not as handsome as Krzysztof.

"Hey," the roommate said.

"Hi," said my date. "Ron, this is . . . sorry, I forgot your name."

I lied, figuring I could backtrack later.

Krzysztof's room was monastically bare. Not messy, not dirty, just bare, nothing on the walls but a plain wooden crucifix. A mattress on the floor. Some of those candles in glass holders decorated with pictures of Jesus and the saints, which Krzysztof went around lighting. A pile of books in one corner, next to a small CD player. An open closet with a handful of clothes on hangers.

"I have to take a pee," Krzysztof said. "Be right back." He closed the door behind himself.

I picked up one of the books. The poems of Saint John

of the Cross. Not the kind of thing I'd find in most of my tricks' rooms. I opened it up, and Krzysztof's name was written on a bookplate inside. *So that's how you spell it,* I thought.

The door opened. "Back," Krzysztof said. He was already pulling off his shirt. Even in the candlelight, I could see how pale he was. There was a flurry of golden-brown hair on his lean chest, a little thicket between large nipples. He never took his eyes off me as he unbuttoned his pants and let them fall to the floor. His briefs had a couple of holes in them. My dick leapt to attention. I put the book down.

Krzysztof walked over to me and dropped to his knees, rubbing his face hard against my crotch, gnawing at my stiff cock through my pants. I grabbed a handful of his candle-light-blond hair and pushed his head into me. He whimpered and squirmed.

"Unzip my fly," I said. He did. "Take my dick out."

"Can I suck it?"

"Not yet. Stand up."

Krzysztof rose to his feet. His torn-up briefs were stretched by his hard-on, the distended holes revealing the pallor of his hip and a flurry of honeyish pubic hair.

"Now turn around." The rest of him was slim, but his ass was perfectly formed, curves and masses beneath the white cotton briefs. There was a tear in the fabric, running halfway down his butt, exposing part of his crack. I went over to him and laid my hand on his ass, and he shivered slightly. I grabbed hold of the cloth with both hands and pulled hard till his briefs gave way with a rip. He trembled even more.

His ass was pale as milk, smooth as silk, beautiful. Most of his body might have verged on the scrawny, but his butt was astonishing. At the top of the cleft, there was a dark tone to his skin, bruise-like, the kind of thing you sometimes see with very pale guys. I ran my fingers over the spot, then down into the crack. He shifted, relaxing so I could slide my fingertips over the moist heat of his hole.

"Okay," I said. "Get down on the bed, on your belly. Keep what's left of those briefs on."

"Yes," he said, lying down, looking expectant, nervous.

"Untie my boots," I said, standing on the mattress to either side of his head. He squirmed around and untied the laces, then pulled my shoes off. He kissed my right foot.

"Now get your butt in the air."

The shreds of white cotton fell away, exposing even whiter ass-cheeks which, slightly parted, revealed a trail of dark blond hair. I reached down and spread his ass. His hole was perfectly shaped, clean, pink and nested in a halo of cinnamon-colored fur, and I wanted it.

"Can I turn on music? My roommate . . ."

"Sure."

He reached over and hit the button on the player. The chanting of medieval nuns. Unbelievable.

There was so much I could have done with Krzysztof. I could have fucked his mouth, his ass. From the look of things, I could have tied him up and beaten him. I could have shown the weedy fucker what a truly demanding top I can be. Didn't, though. I knew then, with the certainty of damnation, that I was going to eat out Krzysztof's ass. His ass. My mouth. Magic. Poison.

I breathed in. Slightly musty but clean.

"What?"

Krzysztof repeated himself. "Yes, please," he said.

The nuns chanted away about salvation or something. I dove face-first into the Eye of God, started at the bruise-dark beginnings of his crack, tonguing flesh against bone, then lower, toward another sort of darkness. My spit matted down the hair. Lower. Lower. Toward the heat. My tongue brushed, just brushed, the soft pucker of flesh, then moved down to the ridge between his furry blond upper thighs, to the base of his balls, my chin resting against the baby-soft sac, the smell of his asshole sweet in my nostrils.

This time I understood what he was muttering into his pillow: "Yes yes yes."

I pulled his perfect ass-cheeks apart and looked down at the now-shiny hole nestled in swirls of damp hair. A hole that led to Krzysztof's guts, to his shit, his heart, his soul, his essence. An Easter egg. Gobble it down.

I spit on my forefinger, rubbed it tentatively around the damp hole, pushed slightly, met initial resistance, then welcome. I sank in to the first knuckle, pulled my finger out, sniffed at it, sucked at my fingertip. My passion. His asshole was my passion. I lowered myself to his butt and stuck my tongue in.

Krzysztof sighed and pushed his ass up at me. I burrowed deeper, tasting the brink of his insides, wanting to go farther, to commit myself utterly to him, to eat my way to wherever he truly was, whoever he was. Krzysztof.

The door opened. The roommate. I gave him a side-long look, then I backed off and spread the pale ass-cheeks so he could see where I'd been. The hole was wide now, shiny, engorged. Licking, kissing, sucking, I dove back inside Krzysztof.

I hadn't thought of my dick for what seemed like a long time. Why would I, when it wasn't my cock but my tongue, my heedless, hungry mouth, that connected me with the risky blond boy lying askew on his barren bed? But now I realized that I'd been leaking pre-cum like a motherfucker, that my cock was slimy-slick inside my pants.

I reared back, kneeling, and brought my hand down hard-on Krzysztof's ass. I didn't want to hurt him; I'm not a sadist. I just wanted to leave my mark on him, the way he was leaving his mark on me, the way I could smell his asshole on my upper lip. The angry-pink print of my hand rose on his very pale flesh, tearing with unexpected ferocity at my heart. I bent over and kissed the mark I'd left, then spread his cheeks and trailed my tongue again toward Krzysztof's musky hole.

"Let me get on my back," he said.

While he rolled over, I looked up at the roommate. Ron. The guy was just standing there, not even touching the hard-on that bulged inside his boxers. I didn't know if he was waiting to be asked to join in or what. I didn't even know whether he was Krzysztof's boyfriend.

"Leave, please," I said. He didn't. I was in no mood to argue with him.

Krzysztof was on his back now, knees up to his chest, his arms looped around his bent legs, ass stretched, open, his hole wet, exposed, his dick stiff against his lean, hairy belly. Nice dick, uncut, dripping, but it was his ass I wanted, needed. I lay on the floor and licked at his asshole, which quivered, responded, opened even wider for my mouth. My tongue strained to go up inside him, as far as I could go. It was all that mattered. I reached up and spread his hole with my thumbs. I had to taste Krzysztof, devour him, be devoured by him, his ass, my desire for him, for his hole, for Krzysztof's ass. The nuns had stopped singing.

"Oh, fuck!" said Krzysztof as I lay there shooting my tongue in and out, flicking it against his secret flesh.

"Have fun," the roommate or boyfriend or whoever said, shutting the door behind himself with a small slam. Whatever. I took my mouth off the deep, dark abyss and looked up, across dick and belly and chest, at Krzysztof's beautiful, blissed-out face.

"What's wrong?" he asked.

"Nothing's wrong," I said, and nothing was. Nothing at all, not in the whole world, a world that smelled like Krzysztof's ass, a world that *was* Krzysztof's ass, a world that was heaven, pure heaven.

He said, "I need to cum soon."

"I want you to sit on my face," I said.

"I can do that."

I tugged off my shirt, pulled my pants down to mid-thigh, scooted onto the mattress and lay on my back. Krzysztof straddled me and squatted down, his butt just inches from my face. I marveled at his ass, its curves, its pallor, even the one small blemish on the left cheek. That blemish made him human; otherwise the perfection of it would have been too much, would have maybe made me cry.

I inhaled his smell again, then stuck out my tongue. He lowered himself onto my mouth and I gobbled at him, starving. I could tell he was jacking himself off; as waves of pleasure rolled through his body, his asshole tightened and expanded, again and again. My world, my universe was his ass, his pleasure, my utter subjugation, my triumph, my access to Krzysztof's ass. Heaven. Heaven. No one who hasn't been there could possibly understand.

He bent over and grabbed my dick. I was too close. I pulled his hand away. Too late—I was going to shoot. I didn't want to, didn't want to leave Krzysztof's ass, not ever, but it was too late. I squirmed, arched upward, burrowed my tongue as far up into him as fate and love allowed, and could feel him pumping away, could feel cum landing on my chest and belly. His cum, my cum, ours.

Some moments are perfect moments. Krzysztof's asshole was a perfect moment. There was nothing, really, to say or do after that. He pulled himself off me and I felt alone. He reached over to the CD player and the nuns started chanting again. He stood, walked to the closet, threw me a towel. I wiped off and got dressed. He wrote his name and phone number down on a slip of paper. When he handed it to me, I didn't offer mine in return.

I knew that in a perfect world, I would have spent the rest of my life rimming Krzysztof's ass, but it isn't, and I wouldn't.

We kissed.

"I can taste my ass on your lips," he said.

"Romantic," I said, and meant it. "I'll show myself out."

I hoped I wouldn't run into his roommate or boyfriend or whatever, and I didn't. When I got outside, I crumpled up the paper with his phone number and let it drop to the gutter. I got to the Jaguar, paused, went back and picked up the paper, smoothed it out, put it in my pocket.

I was glad my Jag was in still in one piece. I was glad to be leaving that part of town. I was even glad, in a way I didn't quite understand, to be driving away from Krzysztof.

Some moments are perfect. Just like that.

Riding With Walter

Greg Wharton

Walter is standing on the seat, his head proudly hanging out the window, his tail wagging with happiness. This is his favorite thing, cruising in my truck with me, teary-eyed in the wind, his muzzle drooling over everything it comes in contact with.

"Where to, huh? What do you say we hit the Dunes today . . . go for a little road trip? Huh, buddy? Got anything better to do?"

I had to get out of the city. Last night was a blur. One fucking blur. I don't know what got into me, what I was thinking. Oh, but I do know. That ass. A perfect ass.

It's not like I haven't looked before. Eddie and I spend a lot of time together. He's my sister's husband. So I've looked, checked out the package every so often. He's very handsome, sexy. I just never thought too much about it. He's married: family. Besides, he always wears big baggy pants.

I pull into traffic, heading west to 94. That will take me out of the city and to the Indiana Dunes. My hair feels grainy as I rub my fingers through it. I didn't bathe when I got up, just brushed my teeth, grabbed my cut-offs, my keys and Walter. Eddie was long gone.

I bring my hand to my face and feel a stirring in my cock as I breathe deep. His smell. All over my hands. His scent so strong on my fingertips: cum, sweat, his ass. Like caramel, sweet caramel. I take a deep breath, swooning at the smell of his ass on my fingers. . . .

Shit! I swerve back into my lane before nearly hitting the car next to me! God, that was close. Walter gives me a look like he knows what I was thinking about, then goes back to hanging out the window, drool and all.

"You were no help at all, you know," I snap at Walter as if last night were his fault.

Last night, shit, last night. I could hardly blame Walter though; ignoring me and sleeping next to Eddie on the bed like it was natural that he was naked in my bed. Like Eddie belonged there. . . .

I knew it was him from the stomps on the steps. His footsteps were unmistakable; always hitting the same creaks loudly every time he visited. The same sounds that no one else seemed to make when they climbed the stairs to my second floor flat. But he did. Every time.

I opened the door before he knocked, happy to see him.

"What's up, Eddie?" My smile quickly dropped once I saw his sad face and puffy red eyes.

"She left, John. She left me. Well, not for good I don't think. Just tonight, she went to your folks'. She's pissed, real pissed. I think I pushed her too far this time."

He cried on my shoulder and I, uncomfortably, did my best to comfort him through four Coronas each, a pack of Camels, and three hours of reruns on Nick-at-Nite. He genuinely didn't understand why my sister was pissed off. He wanted kids, now, and she didn't. Christ, she was just made a partner at her firm. She didn't have time. And I don't think she was ready. But Eddie was old-fashioned Latino, from a large family, and ready for her to pop out some kids.

I finally tired and told him to stay with me instead of driving home. I made up the couch, tucked him in like a five-year-old, and went to bed more than a little tipsy.

I'm not sure what time it was when I had to pee. Tip-toeing through the living room, I made it to the bathroom without a sound. On my way back through, I looked over at my guest. The streetlamps were casting light through the room and caught Eddie asleep on his stomach, the sheet kicked aside and his perfect brown butt-cheeks in full view.

My god, they were perfect! Chiseled mounds of dimpled bubble-butt just staring at me. I froze. He looked so angelic. I could almost imagine billowy white angel wings sprouting from his shoulder blades. A beautiful brown angel asleep on my couch.

Without thinking, my hand went to my cock and I

stroked it through my briefs. He looked so good. So good! I reached inside and wrapped my hand around my growing hard-on, wondering what his cock looked like when I saw *them* move. Not just move; they were flexing. His ass cheeks were flexing. My mind was slow to realize what my eyes were seeing. Then I looked at his face and saw him watching me. Watching me watching him and jerking off!

Oh shit! But he was smiling. A smile unlike any I'd ever seen from Eddie. This one was wicked. Absolutely wicked.

He didn't say anything, just slowly stretched his body out full, then readjusted himself, lifting his ass into the air and reaching under to obviously stroke. His ass-cheeks bobbed in the air as he jerked, calling my name, taunting me.

I didn't think, I just moved. Not to the bedroom as you might assume, but to the couch and straight to his ass. His big beautiful ass that he was obviously offering. I wasn't thinking of Eddie with my sister. My sister didn't exist. Just Eddie. And Eddie's large, muscled ass dancing just inches from my face. And what I intended to do to it.

Before my face even found its target, I heard him moan. Long and deep, as if he were in ecstasy. My cock jerked in its confinement. Then my lips grazed his ass, first up one smooth cheek then the other, until my nose, full of his heavy scent, guided my mouth to the puckered hole. A first date kiss. Gentle and soft at first, then more needy, finally exploring with my tongue. Hungry and deep, as if I hadn't eaten in days and he were a meal. . . .

With one hand on the steering wheel, I unbutton my cut-offs and free my hard cock. I begin stroking hard, trying my best to keep my eyes focused on the road, my pre-cum dripping in anticipation over my fist. I lick my lips, the taste of him still there or possibly just imagined at this point. Oh, Eddie! I pull harder and harder, stretching my cock's skin for all it's worth, my foot pressing against the gas pedal, trying to outrun my desire and last night.

To outrun my thoughts of Eddie.

The first time I came last night, I came without even touching myself. Both my hands were under his body, between his legs, jerking on his thick brown cock as one, my tongue fucking his asshole deeply. When he came, he cried out my name loudly, repeatedly, his ass constricting over and over around my tongue, his cock furiously pumping in my fists. And I came. And came.

What am I gonna do, I think now as my orgasm builds up in my balls. What can I do? Nothing. We'll both pretend it didn't happen. He didn't let me eat his ass out. He didn't let me jerk him off. I didn't lick the cum from his body, didn't kiss his sweet mouth.

"What am I gonna do, Walter?"

We'll pretend that he didn't get hard and cum again, this time inside my mouth. And he didn't stick his large fingers up my ass and finger-fuck me while I shot all over his chest and neck. We didn't fall asleep spooned together on my bed like we were in love. We'll pretend it didn't happen. Maybe we'll just pretend it didn't happen!

When I shoot, my cum splatters all over the wheel and the dashboard. The speedometer reads 85 as I cross the Indiana state line. We're almost to the dunes, the beach and a swim. I relax my foot to a steady 65, and rub my cum into my cutoffs and skin as best as I can.

I'm still hard, so I leave my cock uncovered. I'm still hard and thinking of Eddie. I'm thinking about Eddie and my sister. I'm thinking of Eddie and his sweet ass. His sweet delicious ass. I suck my fingers, pretending they're his. And I'm thinking about what I'm gonna do about the mess I've gotten myself into when I pull into the lot at the beach and park.

But I'm already thinking of when I can taste him again. I need to taste him again. I bring my sticky fingers to my lips.

Walter hasn't moved from his favorite spot standing on the seat, his head proudly hanging out the window, his tail wagging with happiness, teary-eyed from the wind, his muzzle drooling all over the side of my truck.

America's Passion Kings

Troy Ygnacio Soriano

I am smiling. He is smiling. I spin my index finger in a circle.
He chuckles and turns over. I pull down his underwear slowly. His skin is cool, smooth, and almost blindingly lumines-
cent.

He is so eager to be like this with me that it moves me,
honestly affects me and I find I am momentarily disoriented.
I never knew he had an ass like this, not this breathtaking.
Considered this closely, it makes me want to leave right away
and find the nearest sculptors, painters, and poets and bring
them on a pilgrimage to see It, and say, "Here! Here! Go!"

Still, he is the sort of man who is so busy showing the
world the tough, square parts of his body, I'd never imagined
there could be such beautifully round symmetrical parts as

well. Laid out before me, all his sumptuous feast.

It is his own indifference to the attractiveness of his ass that makes it so very exciting for me. I am surprised that his sometimes inhospitable exterior can give way to such abundant tender parts inside; each part contradicting the other, neither dominant enough to negate its counterpart. Mysterious, this male body. Fascinating that on such a consistently jagged and abstract topography, there could be this expanse of secret vulnerability. His secret tenderness. Because he considers himself a strong man only enhances the incongruity. It seemed to me that the tougher, the more masculine the man, the more erotically charged his few vulnerabilities become.

Glancing over his body, from head to toe, his angular, hyper-masculine frame starting off all square units and protruding strength, only falling into curves right after the small of the back. At midpoint, his swinging, pendulous, weighty dick on one side, his incomparably addictive ass on the other, a moment of sacred polarity.

Looking at him completely naked, sprawled regally facedown on the floor in front of the fire, I am suddenly reminded of the athletic de' Medici nudes in Italy. That was the last time I felt such reverence, such knee-buckling inspiration and outright awe. I swallow hard and I can feel my facial hair grow faster. I move his legs far apart and blow on his butthole, tickling him. He laughs and I kiss his asshole affectionately.

His asshole. Lovely, pink, it represents both his

humanity and his divinity. I was very clear on this. I was quite taken with almost every aspect of this beautiful man's asshole. I wanted to see the most vulnerable spot on his body directly, his asshole. I wanted him to show it to me, unguarded and unafraid, opening it for me with his fingers, almost proud.

I didn't want to see his persona, the one he put on show for the world, for his friends, or for his boss. I wanted him to let me see him utterly without armor. There could be no more vulnerable, unprotected and intimate position than in front of me with his back to me, turned away and bent over, spreading his ass-cheeks, his eyes closed, and his hair falling all around.

And a big smile on his face.

In a world where men are taught to battle each other, to jockey for power, to lie, to hurt, to crush each other if they can, to invite another man to fuck your asshole is probably one of the most courageous and liberating things a man can do. And the man that does is not, to me, weak or feminine, nor unintelligent or undignified. He seems rather, on the very far end of all of these. Gracious, sexy, and beautiful.

If you are the man entrusted with another man's very bowels, invited into his very guts for your mutual pleasure and wonderment, how could you not take that to be an honor? What invitation is more total?

My eager dick is so hard, my drooling dickhead has come completely out of the top elastic of my underwear, almost as if it, too, wants to see, wants to appreciate, anticipate and most of all, participate. I run my fingertips ever so lightly over him till he shivers. I run the flat of my palms up and down his back, hard. Overwhelmed by my appetite for him, I press my face against his butt, into his ass, and bite his ass almost menacingly. I will not delay my reward a moment longer, and I part his butt cheeks with my tongue.

Cinnamon and sugar, spicy ginger, his light sweat refreshing like an orange segment. I like that I know all his secret tastes. Eating out his butthole is at first urgent and fast, like heavy metal. Then it's improvisational, around and around, playful, happy like jazz, at its height becoming a professionals-only event, serious, like a full orchestra with a crescendo in mind, till it ends in his utterly low and satisfied Bravo, and I swear I can even hear angels singing. You have some idea of how happy a man I have been, when for sixteen months this is what we have been calling foreplay. . . .

A lot of guys are shy when they take off their clothes in the locker room.

They stumble out of their pants, struggle out of their underwear, leave their clothes on the floor, leave the shower stall in a trance, drop their towels, self-consciously turn around so that no one can check them out. Which is what he did.

An impulse which is itself curiously presumptive: why would anyone be looking at his naked wet muscular body in the men's locker room? Unless he is acutely aware of his own sensual offerings in this crowd? And in this respect, why would hiding his penis, by turning around, not be even more pleasant for his audience? He not only assumed an audience, he assumed a sensualistic preference for this assumed audience.

It's not your princely, handsome, pendulous dick I'm drooling over. If you feel my eyes on you, and you turn away, you end up showing me that round, muscular, soft and inviting ass of yours.

It's like handing me a thousand dollar bill.

Only, his butt is a hell of a lot more than merely inviting. The phrase "fucking relentless" comes to mind.

His ass is just so fucking beautiful! It is much too effective an advertisement for a sex act still illegal in 32 states. I might reflect, that while standing in the check-out line at the grocery store or in some similar place, he had, just in the process of shifting his weight or bending over, probably activated secondary sexual responses in both male and female passersby. His ass spoke of himself and his life, his activities: a hearty diet and a lot of rigorous lifting. Quick sports like soccer, a good amount of walking, and then sitting and having a picnic maybe. Equal parts pleasant meals and hard work, that's what goes into an ass like that.

That he put on his striped oxford first was a disappointment. It's a trick guys do to hide themselves. Sometimes, they'll even put their underwear underneath the towel they have wrapped around their waist, so that at no point are they completely naked in front of everyone. Even straight guys regard this as wimpy.

It's considered strange.

But then he dropped his keys.

Now, whenever I am in an elevator, whenever I am tired or annoyed or bored, when someone is lecturing me or if I am getting bad service at the espresso joint, basically whenever I think that God does not exist, I remember that moment in slow motion. . . .

I start to visit him at his apartment. We are drinking late one evening on his bed and watching television. Due to the amount we are drinking, I have to use the bathroom. Due to the fact that there is no coffee table, I look around and wonder where I should put my full shot glass. Not on the floor, that's how you broke the last one is the response, and so with drunken ingenuity, I tell him that I'll use him as a coffee table and with that, I settle the glass on his back.

When I return, the shot is still there, still full. But I sit down and he looks up at me and smiles at the same time and the shot tips over. We are both caught off guard and disappointed because we are still at the age where alcohol is a precious commodity.

The liquor meanwhile has pooled in the small of his back. I establish eye contact and lean forward in the way that asks: what should I do. He looks cute, almost about to fall asleep and then he says: well, don't waste it. So, I lean forward to suck the elixir, but he moves ever so slightly and it starts to run down his back in little rivers into his butt-crack.

I lick my lips and start sucking it up, and I follow it down. I'm licking the liquor off him and I'm also licking his butt, his butthole. And I'm doing this for what seems like hours.

Was it?

He starts laughing and says with curiosity and with gentleness: "What are you doing?" He turns around and his large dick is hard. I go to kiss him. He is just a bit awkward, but then I do.

And he loves it.

His ankles are on my shoulders. I turn my face to the side and I let my lips and my eyelashes graze the comforting downy hairs on his calves and I've got the cool naked trembling flesh of his ass cupped up in my hands.

All over his arms, up and down his lightly hairy legs, on his round and muscular ass: in one instant and with one gesture, namely by popping my dickhead into his asshole, on all of these sites, I was, in his words, installing the goose bumps.

I see the dark hairs around the bottom of my thick shaft lightly intermingling with the hair around his asshole, and it gives me ice cream for brains. My eyes are rolling around in my head, I'm calling out his name, I'm telling him I love him, over and over, but what I'm thinking is this:

I'd rip up the original copy of the Declaration of Independence for this ass. I'd disown family members for this ass. I'd kill priests and nuns for this ass. I'd sell the Soviets nuclear weapons for this ass.

He has a way of getting fucked that makes me think he's fucking me.

It's sixteen months later, and tonight like an abstract painter, I will be covering his butthole in vanilla ice cream.

He will be drizzling me with maple syrup and I'll be shower-
ing him with whipped cream. Great sex is like enjoying a
great meal. If you're not a mess when it's over, then you did-
n't do it right. And who says you have to clean up right away?

There are certain states of intense pleasure that can
never be known partially.

And yet he knows I love him. For he has worked his
way into my subconscious, where he pleasantly resides
behind all the boring thoughts. Behind my office luncheons
and my appointments, my workouts in the gym, above and
beyond my busy schedule, my ongoing education in an end-
less variety of nothing—there he is, as exquisite, simple and
as necessary as delight can be.

Now, as if it's an exquisite pillow, I fall asleep on his
ass. Or, I fall asleep hard in his ass. I wake up in his ass. I fuck
him, on a floating lounge in the pool, or in the tall green
grass.

I unbutton his shirt and I forget my name. I unbutton
his fly and I break into a sweat. He puts two fingers in my
mouth. I smile. I wrestle with him. I wrestle with my attraction to him. I lick the bottom of his foot and he laughs. He
catches me picking up his jockey shorts off the laundry and
pressing it to my face, and he laughs even harder, but I don't
care.

And I think it was when he was sitting on my face—
and I was pouring honey-almond liqueur all over his body,
massaging it into his back, and it was running down, down,
down, dripping off his butthole into my mouth as he was

grabbing my hair, forcing me deeper into him, and I was noticing his quite radiant skin and the astonishing golden hairs all over his legs and ass and all around his asshole—it was then that I realized I was unspeakably in love with him.

By Sight

Steve Nugent

"Butt . . ." I blurted.

"But what?" Jim asked, looking up from his book, as if detecting some excitement in my voice.

"Oh, nothing. . . ." I mumbled. Jim peered at me and then went back to his reading.

Why had I said that? Of course, I knew why I said it—that guy in the cafeteria. I mean, that butt. It never leaves my churning mind. Like an obsession. I was seeing it again when I said it, and realized that I had a half-formed erection.

I first saw it at around 3pm on Tuesday, the 15th of June.

Its owner is lined up in the staff cafeteria to pay for his coffee. It takes my breath away, a hackneyed phrase I admit, but so true in this case. It protrudes as if it were a shelf on which one could almost rest an object. No underwear, not even a jock-strap or wallet to interrupt the sheerness of that marvelously concise expanse of flesh. So rounded and tidily formed, so proportionate to the rest of the body, it seems to mold itself into his tight black pants, the fine material elastically and smoothly covering the skin beneath (without a wrinkle of a wallet or underwear) as it burrows its way into the crack without a crease, deeply delving, probably arousing his rosebud as he moves. I stare without caution, not bothering, as I usually do on such occasions, to see if I am observed. I had indeed already changed my place at table to get a clearer view.

When he moves slightly, restlessly as he waits, from one foot to the other, the whole configuration changes, the crack momentarily widening at its base, the muscles contracting and stiffening. And how he then flexes those muscles, even tightening his sphincter (oh yes!) as if to reassure himself of the existence of that beauty that he carries so unselfconsciously.

Can he not know the effect it is having on others? Why is the whole cafeteria not focused on this ass? He is surely sent by some sensual God to pleasure me, and to torture me with this exhibition, standing long enough at the counter for me to study him fully. I study his butt, as that particular piece of anatomy makes the rest of him totally irrelevant. I could not care about his general appearance, or even his basket, an area to which I usually pay a great deal of attention.

I want the line to stall or slow down to allow me more

time. What if he comes and sits at my table? A pleasurable shiver of expectation courses through me. He turns from the cashier, hesitates, looks up and down the space and then comes toward me. Now I feel panic, heart thumping, palms moistening, a prospect of catastrophe. I don't want him to sit beside me for I swear I would be heard over-breathing; and if too near me, the sight line will be impaired.

There is a compromise. He sits a few feet away at the next table. Difficult to sight it from here of course, but I can make the most of even that obstruction. His closeness becomes a distraction, forcing me to think more of what may be there than what I can see. I steal lateral glances at how he leans forward as he drinks his coffee, slowly turning the pages of his magazine, moving it on the seat. I slyly glance to the side and see the protrusion of the upper part of his butt, even more pronounced when he sits than when he stands.

I imagine him going home at night to his bedroom, and in front of a full length mirror, slowly stripping. His coat, his tie, his shirt, a T-shirt all come quickly off . . . unbuckling his belt . . . his boxers, the pants slipping to the floor, then nonchalantly kicked aside. His socks peeled off, naked now, he turns this way and that, gazing steadily in the mirror at the defined line of his tan. His hands brush over his buttocks and he parts the cheeks, then bends and admires the curve of his crack. Pulling his ass-cheeks farther apart, he looks back to see his pinkish-brown bud. I'm in the bedroom with him now, standing in the doorway. He half turns and seeing me, beckons me to come in, looking at me with insolence and invitation. I approach, my hand out-stretched to . . .

Then he gets up from the table. Damn, it's like my dreams; I always awaken when the action gets intense. He's now at my elbow and turning his butt toward me, inching his way between the tables, being careful not to touch anything. "Touch *me!*" I want to shout, but he quickly moves out and away, toward the exit. Should I follow him? I want to. He must work somewhere close by.

I jump up from the table, adjusting my cock as I do. I almost run as I see it now moving in a fast, rhythmic way. That great movement of the pelvis, designed by God to insinuate itself with a beautiful mobility to and fro and up and down. He walks ahead, his body swaying from side to side, his thighs exaggeratedly flexing and closing. I'm so close behind him now that I could reach out and touch him, stroke his butt-cheeks. . . .

"I know what you want to do," he will say, unbuckling his belt and dropping his pants and boxers to the floor, pre-senting it fully to me, uninhibited. Then, reaching out to guide my hand to his butt and into his crack, he smiles at me encouragingly. I feel the warm moistness on my fingers. A faint odor of sweat and man rises. I move my face to his crack and my tongue licks his buttocks. Then the tip of my tongue teases his opening and he quivers and moans and urges me to do more. I fondle my hardening cock, and as I suck and smell-taste his ass juices, he pushes out his bud for me to enter him with my tongue. I massage the steely beauty of his globes while my stiff tongue penetrates him. The quickening movement of his ass from side to side demands more, his moaning intensifying with every brush of my tongue. I want to fuck him now, to feel myself in him, pushing up, giving him what I imagine he has always wanted but never dared to demand.

But he is gone again! He quickly turns and moves up the escalator. I follow in time to see him disappear into an office of a bank on the second floor. Gone! I may never see it again. A feeling of panic takes over, combined with my desolation. But I console myself. At least I have a general idea of his location. I will return for that coffee break at the same time tomorrow. It must be there. I must see it again. I must.

At home, Jim stands by the kitchen counter and asks me, as he always does at this time and place, how my day went, and I tell him that it was as usual. Jim turns away with a shrug. He bends over the sink and I see his butt . . . as if for the first time.

"Jim, you've got good-looking buns, you know."

"I know I have. About time you noticed."

I fumble. "There are all your other, more obvious, features that gain my attention."

He turns, laughs, and looks me in the eye.

"I'm sure you've seen better."

"Maybe, but . . ."

I don't complete the sentence. I'm already lost in planning tomorrow's sighting.

Jim's Butt

Jason A. Andresen

The dim light from the hall spilled softly through the bedroom door, across the floor and onto the bed I shared with
my cousin Jim. A small amount splashed onto the ceiling,
helping light my way as I slowly carried out my task. It took
me some twenty minutes to slide Jim's pajama bottoms
down. Had I known how sound asleep Jim was, I could have
gotten this far in half the time.

Jim lay asleep on his side, legs drawn up, his butt facing me, inviting me. I began by inserting two fingers under
the waistband, then waiting to see if my tentative touch woke
him. He didn't stir. I slowly, very slowly, slid the elastic over
his hip. If I had lacked incentive five minutes ago, I didn't
now as I was rewarded with the first glimpse of Jim's butt.
Oh, I'd looked at it before, under his jeans, under his shorts

as he dressed in the mornings. I'd even seen it uncovered—all too briefly—as he returned from the shower in the evenings. I'd seen the small Y dimple at the base of his spine that quickly gave way to a deep but tightly closed cleft, marking where his buttocks pressed together in a graceful outward curve.

But I'd never seen it naked, not this close—just inches away. At this distance and angle, the dim light revealed a soft, sparse covering of fine hair not visible in stronger light.

Jim stirred as I tugged gently to slide the waistband from under the hip pressed against the mattress. This, I knew, would be the most dangerous aspect of fully exposing Jim's butt, and I moved slowly, uncovering more skin inch by slow inch. He stirred again, perhaps unconsciously feeling the cool room air on the newly exposed skin. But this movement—accompanied by a soft, sleepy grunt—worked to my advantage as Jim turned more on his stomach and, yes, even flexed his upper body more toward his belly. I celebrated my good fortune as this pulled his buttocks apart slightly. The rest would be relatively easy. All I had to do was slide his pants down over the remaining half of his buttocks to the crease where butt joins leg, and then enjoy the fruits of my efforts. I forced myself to wait a few seconds until I heard the soft sound of his deep, even breathing again.

Now lay before me a sight I had longed to view. I stared for I'm not sure how long at the beautiful curves, the plump flesh, the deep, dark cleft. Then, emboldened by my success thus far and abandoning all caution, I reached down and touched Jim's butt—ever so lightly. It felt much as I imagined it would: soft yet firm. I ran first one, then two extended fingers up and down the softness from spine to legs, then repeated the motion with four fingers, the tips just brushing the skin.

I leaned forward until my nose was only an inch or so away and inhaled deeply. The gentle, distant aroma of the soap Jim used in his nightly showers was all I could smell, but that was quite enough. It was more the source of the odor, not the odor itself that caused me take in several more deep breathes. I leaned forward the remaining inch and touched my mouth to Jim's butt, not enough to taste but to feel the skin on my lips.

I now took an even bigger chance and slowly slid a finger down into the crevice between Jim's buttocks—ever so slowly—pressing, stopping, then pressing farther. After several misses, at last I found the wrinkled, slippery knot of Jim's anus. I rubbed it gently, not daring to press too hard but very much wanting to. The knuckles of my other fingers press into the flesh as I probe as deeply as I dared.

Jim stirred again, moving his leg only enough to trap my extended finger firmly between his buttocks. I enjoyed the feeling as I again waited for his breathing to resume. Then I slowly slid the finger free and, yes, placed the tip to my nose and breathed in the musky aroma of Jim's butt. I sniffed until there was no aroma left to smell while looking down at where my finger had been.

At last I moved away, pulling the waistband halfway

up, partially hiding my activity. Then I turned to my pillow, lay back and quickly fell asleep, thinking of Jim's butt.

Banff Rim-off

Jay O. Dickingson

The Beef Stroganov is exquisite, prepared the classic Russian way with a mustard and sugar paste blended in a sour cream sauce, the beef cut into tender quarter-inch strips and sautéed with just the right balance of mushrooms and onions. Of course, the rich atmosphere of the Banff Springs Hotel, one of a chain of old railway hotels located in the picturesque Canadian Rocky Mountains, and the ambience of the Banffshire Club, contribute to the meal. What makes the dinner complete, however, is the waiter at whose table I am sitting. He is a young man, possibly a student working his way through college. His complexion is dark, hinting perhaps of a Latin ancestry, and his black hair is gelled and highlighted with a tarnished copper. His tapered white shirt and red vest accent his narrow waist and his tight black slacks display his basket and, to me, the most desirable attribute of a man, his buttocks. He stands about five-foot-nine and has a slender build, a hundred and thirty pounds I estimate. His butt is small, a gorgeous sight that rivals the majesty of the mountains outside.

"And what would you like for dessert, sir?" he asks as he picks up my dirty plate and utensils. "We have a delicious puff pastry with caramelized apple slices, or perhaps a slice of our famous Black Forest Cake?"

"Mmm, no," I reply as I look up at him. God, he has such gorgeous chocolate brown eyes and long, curled eyelashes that many women would kill for. "I'd rather have you. What time do you get off work?"

I actually say it. As the words are slipping off my tongue, I cannot believe it. During the meal, I'd been fantasizing saying that to him and what would transpire. With the amount of traveling and dining out I do, it is not the first time I've had that thought about one of my waiters. It is, however, the first time I've actually voiced such a moronic cliché. That is so unlike me. The kid has to think I am a total idiot. Worse still, I have just put him in the embarrassing position of having to be nice to a diner whom he has to think is an asshole and a lecherous old goat.

"Eleven."

It isn't an apologetic: *I'm sorry, sir, but I don't get off until eleven and then I'll be too tired.* It is not accompanied by a courteous laugh so as to treat my inane comment as a joke to get us both out of a difficult situation. Nor is it a courteous answer while secretly thinking he'd like to cut off my balls with a dull butter knife. It is a simple and sincere, "Eleven."

"That's no problem," I reply in a state of surprise. "I'm in, um, room 512."

"You'd best know up front I'm a top," he whispers as he looks directly at me without a single blink of those beautiful eyelashes.

"That's no problem either," I reply, my mouth forming the words totally independent of my brain, which at the moment is struggling to accept that he's serious.

It is nine o'clock when I leave the dining room. The next two hours are the longest two hours I have ever had to wait, and while I wait, my mind is a continuous jumble of thoughts and worries. Should I change? My clothes are clean, and what else would I wear? Should I shower?

I'd showered just before dining. Besides, I want to smell like me, not like lavender soap. I wonder if he'll show up in his uniform, or if he'll change first. I hope he doesn't change. He looked very sexy in the hotel's waiter's uniform.

I glance at my image in the full-length mirror. At forty-six, my five-foot-eleven frame has put on a few extra pounds, mostly gut and backside, but I am still in reasonably good shape, unlike some of my pear-shaped friends and colleagues of the same age. My dark brown hair has a tinge of gray in the temples, which many former sex partners have said gives me a distinguished look. My steel-gray eyes still have a sparkle in them and age has not yet begun to show in my face.

I wonder if he'll shower before coming to my room, or if he'll ask to use the shower when he arrives. I hope that he comes as he is and we'll have sex first and then shower together. I much prefer the natural aroma of a man than the artificial perfume of soap. As I picture the two of us in the hotel bed, I wonder what his preferred sex act is. He'd made a point of telling me he was a top. As a lover of men's back-sides, I am generally a top also, though not exclusively, and I've had some great sex as a bottom. Whatever he has in mind, I hope that I'll have a chance at enjoying his butt. It will be a most disappointing conclusion to an otherwise wonderful evening if I don't.

Five minutes before eleven, I shave, then sit in the large cushioned chair by the window.

I stare outside at the lamp-lit courtyard and quarter moon reflected in the still mountain lake, but I see nothing as I wait. Suppose he doesn't show? It would not be the first time I'd been stood up, especially by someone his age. When you are twenty, you have many opportunities and many dis-tractions. More than when you are forty-six. When you are twenty, there is always tomorrow or next week or next month. At forty-six, you have to live for now. I'm not saying life is over, but things do slow down, and your choices become more limited. You also become more selective, espe-cially when hitting on strangers for a one-night stand.

That is actually a practice of my past, not my present. As a marketing consultant for Telus Communications, I trav-el a lot, and have established a close network of friends in the major cities of the province and throughout the western United States. If I have a free night, I'll let them know in advance that I'm coming and we'll arrange an evening out, just good friends enjoying each other's company. Sometimes we'll have sex and sometimes we won't. Sex isn't the foundation of many of my relationships. It is a nice extra. That, too, has become more true of my present. It is not something I regret. I am very comfortable with my life.

The rap on my door interrupts my thoughts and causes my heart to leap. It being almost ten years since I've had casual sex with a total stranger, I find my hands embarrassingly clammy and my heartbeat irregular. Suddenly I feel like a young man on the make, except it takes a bit more effort to raise my body out of the overstuffed chair than when I was a young man.

I cross the room and open the door. He is still wearing his waiter's uniform, causing my pulse to quicken and desire to push aside my apprehension. I inhale deeply out of nervousness and I am rewarded with the aromas of the kitchen blended in with the fragrance of a young man.

"Sorry I didn't change," he apologizes as he spreads out his arms and looks down at himself. "I came as soon as we finished cleaning up. Thought I might use your shower if you don't mind. We have to share one over in the staff residences."

"Don't mind at all. You want to use it before or after sex, or during?" I ask with a smile, but it doesn't sound as witty as I'd hoped. It sounds like an inane comment from a desperate, lecherous forty-six-year-old.

"Depends on what you like," he replies with a grin, a slight smile that just curls the corners of his lips and narrows those delightful, sexy eyes. "I'm easy any way."

"Afterward then," I say as I step up to the dresser. "Would you care for a glass of wine? I have some chilled."

"Mukuzani Number Four?"

"Yes," I respond in surprise.

"That's what you were drinking with your meal," he explains.

"Hmm, a man of habit am I." I remove the cork and pour us both a glass of the dry red Georgian wine.

"Besides having good taste," he responds as he accepts the glass, "it was an excellent choice with the Stroganov."

"Thanks," I motion for him to sit on the bed while I take the large, padded chair. "I have to ask. What prompted you to take me up on my offer, Derek?"

It is his turn to look at me in surprise for a moment until he realizes he is still wearing his nametag and remembers he'd introduced himself when he'd come to take my order.

"My name is Ray, by the way," I say, extending my hand. He takes it and we shake. It is very formal and stilted, a handshake between strangers, not between two men about to engage in sex.

"So, do I jump into bed with just any diner you mean?" he asks. His chocolate brown eyes twinkle with a humor and an openness, the kind that draws me to the company of young men.

"Well, I wouldn't have put it that bluntly," I respond, smiling back as I take a sip of wine.

"The truth is, I work evenings six days a week from four to eleven. Doesn't do anything for my social life."

"I can see why."

"I can drive into Calgary of course. It's only a bit more than an hour. But the idea is to save money for my next year at the U of C, and you don't save money driving with the way gas prices are in this province, especially this summer."

"So what you're saying is that you're taking me up on my offer because you're horny," I observe with a smile as I take another sip, trying to act sophisticated but inside quivering like an aspen. It has been too long since I've done this. I am out of practice and casual sex is a lot more dangerous than when I was his age, but his ass is so attractive. To let something that beautiful go by without even an attempt to worship it would be something I'd regret for weeks to come.

He laughs. It is a genuine laugh, not the laugh a waiter gives at dinner or the laugh of a young man out of respect for an elder. Or of a whore about to service a john.

"In part," he says. "But I'm choosy, and I figure you are, too."

"Oh yes," I admit, admiring his straightforwardness as well as his good looks and his lithe body.

"I figured so," he responds as he downs the rest of his wine. Like most young people, he treats it as a drink, as he would a Coors Light or can of Pepsi, not something to be savored and enjoyed gradually. "So, you want to get it on now?"

Also like most young people, he lives for now and is impatient to begin. "Sure," I respond, putting down my half-empty glass. "Do you have anything in particular in mind?"

"No. But as I said in the dining room, I am a top."

"I hope that doesn't preclude any foreplay with your butt."

"No, but I have a virgin ass and plan on keeping it that way," he responds with a leer and a look of confidence. I want to rip off his clothes and ravage his buttocks regardless of what he wants, but that isn't something I'd ever do.

"Would you consider having it penetrated by my tongue as violating your virginity?" I ask as I rise and sit down beside him on the bed. It sinks embarrassingly low under my weight.

"No," he replies, looking directly into my eyes. "I've never been rimmed before actually."

"Well," I reach up and undo the top button of his vest while continuing to stare into his eyes, "this will be the last night you'll ever be able to say that."

He sits there passively as I unbutton his vest and then his white shirt. He is wearing one of those bow ties with the elastic band that fits under your collar. I leave it on as I slip his shirt out from under it and remove the shirt and his vest. He isn't wearing a T underneath and I inhale deeply as my fingertips touch his smooth, muscular body. He has a tuft of black hairs at the V of his neck and circlets of fine hairs about his small, dime-sized teats. The rest of his beautiful chest is sparsely haired.

I run my fingertips between his breasts and trace the fine line of hair that extends down over his ribs before disappearing under his belt. He then reaches up, unbuttons my shirt and slides it off my shoulders. I raise my arms and he rolls my T-shirt up and slips it over my head. Reaching out, he runs his fingers through my thick matte of chest hair, still dark brown but with a sprinkle of gray across the top. He toys with my nipples, larger and more prominent than his. They burn pleasantly as he runs his fingertips in circles around them, then through the circle of hairs surrounding each bud. Finally he gently tweaks them and caresses them, causing them to quickly grow firm. He is a top man and remarkably skilled for his age.

Often the step between the initial conversation and the decision to disrobe is an awkward one, but ours is smooth and natural. I'm feeling good and I can tell he is also. When two men have chosen to disrobe each other, as we have, the lowering of one's trousers is the next big hurdle to be overcome. Does one draw his partner along with him as he casually lays down and raises his hips, or does one interrupt his partner and stand up? Does one take over the task himself at that point, or force his partner into unnatural contortions as he struggles first with the fly, then the drawing down of the trousers and maneuvering them over his partner's feet?

Taking the lead, Derek motions for me to stand. He reaches up and pulls down my fly and undoes my buckle. Drawing down my trousers, he unties my shoes and slips them off. Then as I raise each foot, he slips off my pants one leg at a time. Reaching back up, he draws down my Sears-brand plaid boxers, and again as I raise each foot, he slips them off, along with my socks. I study his face to see his reaction now that he has exposed my manhood, but I detect no response.

The boy being a top man, that is not his primary interest, I know, but I'd hoped for at least some reaction. At four inches flaccid and seven hard, I know I'm larger than the average man and former partners have told me my cock has a nice color and shape, both flaccid and erect.

We switch positions and the anticipation of revealing his beautiful backside sweeps aside my moment of disappointment. I pull down the fly of his black slacks and undo the snap above the zipper. With his narrow waist and his tight slacks, he does not need a belt to keep his slacks up. I ease them down his slender, muscular thighs and finely haired calves. His highly polished shoes are slip-ons and I easily remove them and draw off his slacks, taking his socks with them. Sitting there on the bed, I look up at the young Rocky Mountain stud muffin standing there in his black bow tie and navy blue Fruit of the Loom briefs.

Reaching up and slipping my hands under the elastic band of his underwear, I slowly draw them down and off. I then have him lie down on the bed on his back. I grab his feet and raise them, crawling beneath him until the small of his back is resting against my chest and his legs fold over his head until his feet are resting on the headboard of the bed.

He has a beautiful ass, just as I had thought, smooth and compact. I run my fingers over it reverently, kneading his firm flesh. As he looks up between his legs and watches, I lower my head and inhale the pure male fragrance of his balls, and then of that enticing rosebud.

Starting at his tail bone, I run a finger along his crack, delighting in its slightly oily feel. I pause at his butthole and caress it gently with concentric circles. Not accustomed to receiving attention, it is delightfully sensitive and quivers with my touch. I stroke it more firmly and his cock begins to swell with arousal.

Lowering my head, I sniff at that back portal once again, delighting in the musky fragrance. I stick out my tongue and run it along the same course as my finger had taken, beginning at his tail bone and running along the length of his crack, but I do not pause at his hole.

Instead, I continue up and along the cord running from his asshole to the base of his balls. His cock stretches out for his face as it rapidly swells in response to my foreplay. I lick his crack in reverse and he squirms and his cock swells further.

"Oh man, that feels weird," he sighs.

Spreading apart his firm buns, I place my lips against his asshole and kiss it, and with my lips still firmly pressed against the quivering pucker, I suck in as I would if I were kissing his lips.

Drawing his anal pucker into my eager mouth, my tongue attacks, licking it and striking at it as the tongue of a snake would. He whimpers with the new, erotic sensation. I attack more fiercely, sucking still deeper, creating a vacuum between us that cannot be broken, and I worm my tongue into his dank opening.

"Oh, God," he whispers with a sigh.

Running my lips over the sensitive, firm mounds, just barely touching them, I kiss them gently and repeatedly, tiny pecks of love, pecks of a devout ass worshipper. I notice his cock is fully erect and a clear droplet of pre-cum has formed at the tip. As tempting as that morsel is, I ignore it and return to his anxiously awaiting hole.

"Push out," I whisper, looking past his large, hairy balls and down along his quivering cock and into his eyes. His chocolate brown eyes are half closed with sensual pleasure and his lips are parted and moist from his licking of them. He smiles back up at me knowingly, probably having asked countless partners to do that for the same reason, but a penetration of a far different nature.

As I eagerly fasten my leech lips about his hole again and suck his pucker back into my mouth, I once again wiggle the tip of my tongue into the opening. This time though, he is pushing out, forcing his sphincter open, and my tongue presses into that tiny O-ring and keeps it open. He pants and grunts as he pushes out, and I continue to stretch my tongue out. I've plenty of practice at this and my oral muscle is well up to the task. Deeper and deeper it probes, reaching past the straining sphincter to reach the moist, dank chamber beyond. I wiggle the tip and then dart my tongue in and out of the musky cavity, my saliva flowing abundantly with the delightful flavor of wild mushroom assaulting my tongue. My saliva drains down into his rectum, filling it as another man might wish to fill it with juices of another kind.

Spreading apart his cheeks, I drool directly into his open hole. I know he can feel my spittle trickling into his rectum, and as he gasps and inhales sharply, I know I have him on the brink of cumming. Pressing my lips still tighter against his portal, I blow into it, filling it with my breath as I tease his quivering anus with my tongue, and then once again I force my oral muscle into him.

"Oh fuck," he sighs. His body trembles violently as his cock jerks in the air and his groin erupts in that volcanic ecstasy that is the pinnacle of a man's lust. His cum shoots out of his cock like the hot ash from a volcano. The stiff, aroused organ jerks wildly as it spews out his seed and spatters his body. Thick, creamy cum strikes him in the face and runs in hot rivulets down his cheeks. It lands in the fine hairs in the V below his neck where it sticks as a glob, narrowly missing his bow tie, and it spatters his right nipple and his left breast.

His asshole grasps my tongue as he climaxes, gripping onto it as if using it for an anchor while his body heaves in ecstasy. Shot after shot erupts from his tight balls until finally, the force subsides. His cum, now a stream of hot lava, pours out of his irritated, burning cock slit, forming a puddle in his belly button. I watch as it overflows and creeps along the ribbon of hair I'd followed earlier across his ribs. It flows toward his chest opposite to the direction my fingertips had taken.

Finally the flow subsides and a pendant of cum hangs from his still stiff cock. I wait until his breathing becomes less labored, then slowly remove my tongue, just as spent as he is. I kneel there motionlessly, allowing the pleasure to flow over the two of us, delighting in his orgasm as though it was my own. Finally giving his pucker one last kiss, I lower that beautiful backside back down onto the bed, and I lay beside him, the taste of him in my mouth. I close my eyes and savor the unique bliss of what has been an exquisite rim-off. I'm glad now I asked for dessert, and as he exhales deeply beside me, I know he is too.

A Flame of Flesh . . . for Eric

Adam Ben-Hur

You arrive at my place after work, just a little after sunset. I answer the door naked and smiling, happy to see you. The house is lit with candles and smells of some pleasant spice. Quiet music of flutes and harps plays softly in the background. I pour you a dark German beer and ask how your week has been while you strip off your clothes and slip into the shower. I enjoy the sight of your nakedness and admire the masculine way you move as you undress, completely at ease with yourself, the graceful symmetry of your figure illuminated by the flickering light.

Your body tingles as the warm shower caresses you. You lather your skin with an herbal body lotion, inhaling the fresh, natural fragrance of woods and flowers. As you step out of the shower, glowing pinkly, I unfold a pale, sky-blue towel and dry your broad shouldered back, your round hard buttocks and your powerful legs. Your beautiful cock begins to pulse and lengthen as a smile of pleasure and anticipation opens your face and brings a light to your eyes.

I lead you to the bedroom where you stretch out across the flannel covers of the bed on your belly. Your arms spread wide and your hands reach out and grasp the soft pillows. Your head rests to the left and I hear you sigh a long breath, exhaling the day's tension. I gently open your legs wider and pull your cock back between your legs so the sensitive underside of the shaft and head are exposed to my touch. Beside the bed, a small, oriental, blue and white ceramic bowl contains a warm oil. Dipping my hands into the oil, I begin to massage your back, enjoying the sight of candlelight flickering across your supple and shining skin. You sink more deeply into the bed, breathing quietly.

My hands flow down your back into the curve of your waist, appreciating each muscle and shape. As my hands cross your ass, I gently part the two halves of your buttocks and caress the sensitive inner flesh of your anus, letting the oil flow into the dark moist crevice and down across your testicles. I calmly pass the oil over your cock and am excited to feel the weight and thickness of your erection. The head of your proud cock is swollen with desire and you moan quietly under my touch, opening your legs as far as possible to give me greater access to your sex. I bend forward and slowly drag my tongue across the head of your cock, licking the fat shaft, the meaty, oval balls, and moving slowly up the pronounced seam of your scrotum toward the dark center of pleasure.

As my tongue crosses the lips of your asshole, you reach your hands back and grab both halves of your ass to open them wider for my exploring mouth. Softly, you moan, "oh, God" to let me know a wave of pleasure is washing over your nervous system. Your hips twist and thrust slightly forward in a slow fucking motion as the ecstatic male animal in you emerges from deep inside. My hands fold around your cock as my tongue probes the secret rim of your anus, searching for the nerve switch that releases powerful sexual electricity throughout your body and mind. You moan deeper and longer. You stretch your arms out wide and grasp the bed hard, tensing as the physical pleasure becomes unbearable.

You whisper: "Adam, please fuck me . . . please." And I smile, feeling the heat and heaviness of my Italian cock pressing up against my belly, primed by the sounds and motions of your body. In time with the slow rhythm of the music, I glide forward, bracing my palms on either side of you. I allow my fully erect cock to graze teasingly against the slope of your ass as I move forward and lower myself close to your ear. For a moment, I pause and admire the brave square cut of your jaw and the beautiful way your hair nestles against the back of your neck.

I whisper, "Relax . . . let's just float for a while. I want you to have whatever you want from me, but for now let me adore your perfect ass. There's nothing like this feeling. I know that you need this as much as I need to give it."

You smile and close your eyes, surrendering completely to the embrace and gravity of the bed. An involuntary shudder of pleasure ripples through your body. I glide back to the kneeling position behind your legs. Giving in to my desire to merge more completely with you, I stretch out my legs behind me and bury my face unashamedly in the moist firm flesh of your butt as you strain to open to even greater enjoyment. You reach back and take both my hands in yours, squeezing tightly and telegraphing the intensity of your feelings through our interlaced fingers, as if we are acrobats saving each other from a fall from a great height.

The sound of ocean waves plays through the recording on the stereo. I feel as if I am surfing through some neural tide of bliss, riding a current of pleasure that seems to have no specific source or point of origin. I no longer sense any difference between my lips and tongue and the openings and organs of your body. Your ass seems to know intuitively how to fuck my tongue. My broad, square chin nestles and brushes playfully against your scrotum. In long, leisurely strokes, I return to licking your cock and balls and ass, pressing as deeply as possible with each passage across your asshole . . . lightening up as I near the tender sweet folds of fragrant wet skin that lead to your manhood.

At last, we both realize my tongue can only provide a portion of your true erotic desires. Disengaging with you only long enough to refill your beer and provide myself with the proper protection, I return to the bed. I pause for a moment to enjoy the sight of you naked and spread out wide for me. You seem to be floating in a timeless place. You know what's coming next and begin to raise and tense your buttocks in expectation. I remind you to relax and keep breathing deeply even though it's only natural to tense up. I position my fat hard cock at the portal of your asshole, leaning over to kiss the back of your neck. I remind you that I would never hurt you and that we'll go very slowly. You rise up slightly to meet me and welcome me into the warm dark sheath of your lower colon. I press forward gently, savoring the satisfying pleasure in every centimeter of contact as your powerful sphincter muscle opens to receive my hardness. I bury my cock deep inside you. It feels like coming home. You moan, but it's a sound signaling fulfillment, not pain. I leave my cock in, motionless as you reach back with your ass and squeeze hard several times. Then, gradually, as you adjust to the fuller feeling of penetration, you begin to provide us with the right tempo and depth of ass-fucking motion as I twist my hips from side to side to ensure every nerve of your ass is included in our joining.

You begin to moan. You bury your face into the pillow. You say breathlessly, from some great depth: "Oh, God, fuck me hard, Adam. Please fuck me really hard. It feels great. I really need this right now. Oh God, you're really fucking me hard now." All of my consciousness is now focused deep in my penis, which feels as if it is on fire. I begin to feel the electrical tingle of pre-orgasm sensations from deep inside my body. My balls are pressing up against my scrotum tightly, loaded with the life-giving fluid I've saved up all week for this time alone with you.

The raw erotic creature in my soul knows that I am giving you total, unalloyed pleasure, and my own primordial fucking instincts take over. I am fucking you deep and hard now. The bed rocks. I bend over and bite the back of your neck and start licking and sucking as much of your exposed ear as I can gather in my mouth. You try to turn your head and kiss me, your tongue searching for mine in the candle-lit haze. I raise myself on my hands and lock my elbows, bracing myself for the inevitable. Involuntarily, my knees push your legs as far apart as possible and an excited gasp of breath lets me know I am thrust as deep and far inside you as you needed. Losing control, I fuck hard and fast now as you buck in response like a magnificent animal.

As you begin to climax, I feel the valve of your prostate gland pumping against the underside of my cock, and my own orgasmic roller coaster begins to flow through me, setting off fireworks in my head and heart. My semen gushes powerfully through the entire length of my sex. I moan and continue to fuck you until every drop of semen has been released, spasm by spasm, from that mysterious inner reservoir. I lean forward and embrace your back, enjoying a sense of accomplishment. I let my cock slowly return to normal size inside you as you seem to drift into unconsciousness and peace. You begin to breathe deeply and calmly. I watch you as you drift into a pleasant, tentative after-sex sleep. The stress and tensions of work are a million miles away.

I take the pale sky-blue towel and wipe some of the oil and sweat from your body. I lie down next to you and enjoy a feeling of repose, soaking in the atmosphere of desire fulfilled. I close my eyes, my mind completely free of all thoughts. In a little while you return to earth and I ask you if you'd like to shower again.

"No," you say. "I'll shower when I get home."

I know that you are floating in an altered state of consciousness, so I let you dress in peace.

Before you leave, I give you a hug. Your body feels completely surrendered and vulnerable in my arms.

You smile and say, "Thanks. That was great, Adam!"

I smile, knowing there really isn't a lot to say at times like this. It's just knowing that there is another guy on earth you can open up to and be natural with for a little while that makes a big difference. It's knowing there is a place where you don't need to project any sort of image or facade, where you can just enjoy yourself and explore your most intimate feelings and sensations with another friend.

I think to myself:

I should write a description of this. It may help to open someone's mind a little wider, or lift their heart a little higher. Maybe, deep inside, we are all the same person, the same pure life force seeking only to love and be loved away from the scrutiny and judgment of the world. In private moments of sexual kindness, giving and receiving without fear or shame, some of the sweetness and passion that the humdrum world attempts to take from us returns, making us strong and whole again.

I walk toward the calm blue screen of my computer and begin to write.

A Transitory Encounter

Jamie Anderson

I like living in London, but it does have its drawbacks and I was right in the middle of one: a packed Underground car during rush hour. The dreaded Northern line to be precise. The car, if the date on the casting by the double doors was to be believed, was older than me. God, I hope I'm in better condition when I reach its age. It wheezed and groaned its way south toward central London. We rattled out of the tunnel and into a station where we stopped. The doors hissed open. Three people got out and about thirty pushed in. I hung onto the pole and prayed for patience. I had a newspaper, but it was too crowded for me to open it, let alone read it.

The doors closed, opened, closed and finally opened again. This had been happening at every stop. It usually took about six goes to get all the doors on the train to shut at the same time. While they were open, a foxy little number slipped in and managed to find a place near me. Because of the crush, it was difficult to get a good look at him. I was about a head taller and he was wearing a T-shirt and jeans; but both were so baggy that they totally hid his figure. However I could see that he had dark brown hair, brown eyes, sensuous lips—oh, and there was a little tuft of hair peeping over the neckband of his T-shirt. He looked as though he would go like a little two-stroke once you got him started.

To my horror, I realized that he had caught me giving him the once over. He smiled while I went as red as a beet. The doors cycled a couple of times and some more people pushed in. By some dainty wriggling on his part, he ended up facing me. He gave me a dazzling smile. I returned a sort of guilty lopsided grin.

The doors shut and miraculously stayed closed. The train gave a lurch. There was the loud bang of the traction power overload trip opening and immediately the brakes came full on. Everyone who was not seated got thrown around. I ended up pressed hard against the partition and he was sort of "body slammed" into me. He grabbed me for support, but didn't let go. Then he ground his hips against mine. It was a very small movement but there was no way it could be taken as accidental. He looked up at me, smiled, then licked his lips. A shiver went right through me.

Cocks have a mind of their own—well, mine does. Finding itself rubbed up against someone I fancied, and getting an obvious come-on signal, it began to wake up. The slight humping motion was repeated and things down there really began to stir. The damned doors opened and shut twice more, then the train dragged itself out of the station and into the tunnel.

Taking advantage of the movement of the train, he quickly completed his self appointed task of getting me hard. His hand felt out my manhood and caressed it through the fabric of my lightweight summer suit. Gingerly, I ran my free hand round to his butt. God it was fantastic! Two perfect spheres of muscle and he twitched them for me. I slid my hand up his back and then down again, but this time on the inside of his jeans. I found the waistband of his underwear and went inside it. There was a hairy patch just at the base of his spine, a regular little bear cub.

The train lurched to a stop in the tunnel and we had to cool it for a while. He just held my cock and I rested my hand on his naked butt. We smiled at each other just as the lights flickered and went out. Dim emergency lamps came on at the far ends of the car. Power loss is unusual on the underground and it caused quite a stir. People actually began to talk to each other. A hand slipped round the back of my head pulling it down and forwards. Two lips met mine and we kissed. He squeezed my cock and stuck his tongue in my mouth. I got a finger in the crack of his butt and went for his ring, which I rubbed until he let me in. We broke the kiss and then had a giggle fit.

The situation was bordering on the farcical. There we were in a darkened tube train, all but having sex, completely surrounded by straights who had no idea what was happening. God, if we tried this sort of trick in a gay club, we would be noticed immediately. I wiggled my finger around in his butt, teasing his ring open. I take a perverse delight in fingering another guy's butt, sort of physically violating the privacy of his body. His butt just begged to have a cock in it. He wasn't too tight and I'll bet he could have taken me on spit alone. The lights came on and the train began to move again.

We rolled into the next station and a handful of people got off as several dozen squeezed in. We were now trapped in a corner between the off-side door and the partition. We gently played with each other as the doors did their trick again. As we lurched back into the tunnel, I got a second finger into him and he gave my cock an extra squeeze in appreciation.

At the next stop, more people got out than got on and we had a bit of room to move. He released my manhood, motioned me to pull my hand out, which I did, and then he turned round. I quietly sniffed my fingers and enjoyed the musky male odour on them. He pressed his butt into my crotch. My raging cock was now pressed into firmness of his butt, running right up the crack of it. The bastard began to rub that sensuous butt of his against me. The train shuddered to a halt again and he once more had to cool it.

I reached round and slid my hand under his T-shirt. I found a dense mat of hair round his navel which I followed down, inside his clothing, until I ran across the tip of his cock. It was wet. I worked his foreskin down and rubbed my thumb over the slit. The pre-cum oozed out of him. The train began to roll again and he now humped his butt up and down my cock with a vengeance. I retaliated by sensuously working his cock over. Now the pre-cum was flowing freely and everything in there was getting rather moist. Oh God, his butt was making me so hot.

"You're going to make me shoot if you keep doing that," I breathed in his ear.

The bastard giggled and redoubled his efforts. The train was on his side as it picked up speed and the violent lurching covered his movements. So there, below the streets of London, in a crowded tube train, I had a massive orgasm, all over my underpants! I wanted to scream at the top of my voice, but I could only allow myself a very quiet moan in his ear. I was expecting him to giggle, but he was strangely silent. Then his cock bucked and the warm wet feeling of a male orgasm erupted in my hand.

Vindictively I wiped most of his cum off on his bush before I pulled my hand out. The train stopped again and I was able to get a hanky out of my pocket and surreptitiously clean my hand. His cum smelt nice. I got one of my cards out and slipped it into his hand just as the train started up and rolled into a station. He winked at me and got off.

That was this morning. I haven't been able to get any work done. I just sit in front of my computer, writing this, dreaming of getting him alone and giving that butt of his the attention it deserves. However I must go now as my phone is ringing.

It might be him.

Juicyfruit

James Earl Hardy

a banana split
separating a round
ripe
shiny
smooth
hard
huge
landscape
an immaculate garden
a field of nocturnal dreams

perched ebony palisade
caramel chestnut colony
cinnamon apple acre
brown sugah-ry slope
heavenly Hershey hamlet

maple honey mo'-azz-es

the eighth and ninth wonder of the world
so mountainous
so majestic
so . . .
it's almost insurmountable
(that's right . . . almost)

i'll be like Moses
parting the Red Sea
peach fuzz grazing my nose
tickling my lips
inhaling
ingesting
indulging in
sweet sweat
minty musk
freaky funk

don't tighten up
just pucker up
that pretty pit of a plum

i'm gonna scoop up
and spoon out
a whole lota sumthin sumthin
dive inside
and drown myself

Baskin & Robbins can't make flavas
that tease my tongue
explode in my mouth
coat my throat
and fill my belly
like . . .

strawberry surprise
cherry cheer
raspberry rain
blueberry bomb
mango madness
pineapple punch
tangerine twist
lemon-lime lush
papaya passion
grape gumbo
melon mambo
apricot almond
raisin rum
orange oasis

no whipped cream
sprinkles
or hot fudge
necessary

a sticky wicked treat
so suck-ulent
so d-vine
i gotta thank the Divine
for such a blessing

i done found my religion
unspeakable joy
between another brutha's cheeks

HavMercy!

if my mama only knew
how much i love eatin' fruit
today

On A Sunday Afternoon

Tama Wise

They wrote songs about Sundays this perfect.

Jason tried to remember off the top of his head that song he used to always listen to. Something about Sunday afternoons. He remembered the lead rapper, a smooth, fine looking Latino who looked and sounded about as good as this afternoon felt. Riding aimlessly on his bike, Jason could feel every smooth tone of that song. He could see what would have prompted someone to write about Sundays.

For the lanky teenager, things couldn't get better than this.

Taking a sharp turn over the broken sidewalk, Jason pulled his dirt bike into the next street. His friends were playing pick-up basketball back at their usual hangout, but Jason

just felt like cruising for awhile—doing nothing in particular, going nowhere. A perfect use of an afternoon as perfect
as this.

Despite his slow, coasting speed, he had ended up
some distance from his regular haunts. He peddled languid-
ly, his wanderings taking him down yet another street of tenements. This one was dotted with tall trees that hung over
the sidewalk and road, sheltering all below in their lush green
arms. Still, every now and then, Jason could still feel the sun
as it peeked through the leaves.

As far as he was from home, the places here never
changed. Still the same old ghettos he'd grown up in in
Bradford. He could probably ride a long time and still see the
same sights: kids playing outside on the sidewalks, bruthas
hanging and talking out on the steps. The sun and warmth
made him reminiscence like that. Wearing a black, raid-style
vest, a Razorbacks jersey (as much as the local team was shit,
he supported them), and baggy black shorts, Jason felt the
light breeze caress his bare, light skin and all but bald head
and thought to himself:

How could an afternoon get better than this?

He pulled into the next street, coasting into what
looked like yet another row of tenements. He could have
been riding around in circles for all he knew. Drunk to the
effects of the lazy afternoon sun. He felt no sense of urgency
until . . .

He noticed someone near the steps of one of the tenements. Nothing strange there, but the guy was good-looking

enough to catch his eye. He looked Puerto Rican perhaps.
Smooth dark skin. His hair as short-shaved as Jason's.

Jason's eyes wandered down the guy's body, taking in
what looked like a very athletic frame covered by a baggy
black T-shirt, which was sleeveless and showed off his almost
perfect arms. Jason muttered silent, unheard praise to the
sight before him. His eyes roamed over the Rican's firm pecs
and the rest of his body. Then Jason lowered his glance, taking in the guy's long, loose, black basketball shorts. Where
they ended just below his knees, toned legs emerged.

Jason found himself in slow motion, appreciating the
smooth curves, all things leading him to one question, one
burning fact that he still wanted proven.

A guy as fine as that *had* to have one hell of a butt.

The Rican began to turn around to glance up at the
tenements. Caught up in anticipation, Jason's eyes locked on
the inevitable. . . .

Bam!

There you go!

Jason all but panted as he stared at the guy's rear.
Nothing could be more perfect than what he saw. The
Rican's long black T-shirt even snagged on the waistband of
his basketball shorts. The soft material of the shorts fell
down over the firm, rounded slopes of his ass, thicker and
more prominent than any other part of his body. Jason
couldn't have cared what the rest of him looked like, given
how full his ass looked.

The guy put his foot down on one of the steps and

bent to tie his shoe. The action pulled the smooth fabric of his shorts over the two strong mounds of his butt, hinting at the perfect crack between.

Instantly, Jason brought his bike to a halt and dismounted.

Call it stupidity. Maybe it was the heat of the afternoon. Maybe it was the magic that seemed to hold the whole street in some fairytale-like state. Whatever it was, Jason barely paused a moment between seeing heaven and moving to speak to the angel who had led him there. He walked his bike across the road, his eyes still fixed firmly on ass. He reached his destination just as the guy stood up straight and turned and noticed him.

Their eyes met. Oh, what a pretty face.

This has to be a dream.

There was only one thing to utter.

"I gotta say, bro, you have the fucking finest ass I've ever seen."

Jason held himself against his bike, waiting for the words to sink in and take whatever effect they would on the Rican. He kept his hands on his handlebar rather than look like he was ready to pounce and come off like a complete freak.

The guy had a look of surprise on his face, then chuckled, all but grinning it off.

"No, I'm serious. You work out, right?"

The guy gave him a once over, then pointed at a basketball at the foot of the stairs.

"I ball, that's about it. Lift a few weights." His voice was pretty nice, too.

"You know, basketball is the best sport for butt," Jason said. He rested his bike against the steps of the tenement, noticing the guy's smooth smile.

"Oh yeah, why's that?"

"It's them shorts," Jason explained. "They show off everything a guy got to show." He tried to get another look, still finding it hard to keep his eyes anywhere else. "And bro, you got plenty to show."

"You got guts," the Rican replied. "Not many guys'll go up to a brutha and say that kind of shit to them."

Jason smiled. His mind was abuzz. He hoped the Rican didn't see the bulge in his shorts.

"Name's Ruben." The Rican put out his hand.

"Jason." They shook hands three different ways—ghetto-style.

"So what you up to?" Ruben then asked. "Other than checking out brutha's asses."

Jason shrugged, smiling sheepishly. "Not much, bro. I was just cruising—I mean, not like that . . . just out riding, that is." He motioned toward his bike, trying to make his point better. "My bike—my homies are balling back at my court. I felt like taking a ride for a bit. Catch some air."

"Yeah, where you ball?"

"Back over on 3rd and 12th."

"Oh, yeah? I've played there a few times."

Jason grinned, unable to resist. "I'm there a lot. I

would have remembered someone with an ass as nice as yours." He knew he was a dog. No one else would have pulled a stunt like this one. "Nah, I don't recognize your face . . . turn around."

Ruben scoffed. "You a damned freak, man."

After their laughter faded, there was an awkward pause. Then Ruben checked his watch and said: "Hell, if you ain't going nowhere, come on up to my place, catch a cold drink."

"*Aiiright.*"

Ruben nodded to the bike. "You can bring that up."

Jason was barely able to suppress what he wanted to say next. Thankfully, either Ruben second guessed him or was all too happy to *lead the way*. As he did, Jason stood at the bottom of the stairs. Watching. Unable to get over how well those shorts hung. He did catch himself in time to start following before Ruben turned and wondered where he'd got too.

The hallway on the first floor was cooler than the sidewalk had been. Jason walked his bike down to where the Rican was already unlocking the door, then nodded thanks as Ruben pushed open the door and motioned for him to head on in.

"Excuse the mess," Ruben said, closing the door behind them. "Just dump the bike anywhere."

Jason glanced around the apartment, which was small but comfortable. Two large, far-too-soft-looking couches sat near a small TV and VCR. The place didn't look too bad for this side of town. And judging by the posters on the wall, Ruben sure liked basketball. Vince Carter. Damon Stouda-mire. Brian Grant.

"Oh, yeah, he's good," Jason said, pointing at Brian Grant.

Ruben went into the small kitchen, taking out some tall glasses from an overhead cupboard. "He's having a good season," he said. "Too bad they traded everybody though."

"Just means he has to work harder," Jason said. "Nothing wrong with that. Also means we get to see more of him."

"Water cool?"

"Cool." Jason rested his bike against one of the couch-es and sat down on the other. A large poster of Corey Maggette was on the opposite wall. Ruben came from the kitchen, glasses in hand. He handed one to Jason.

"You saying basketball is a good sport for butt? How you figure that one?" Ruben sat down on the floor, opposite Jason. "I would have thought football was better."

"Football's nice for them tights and all," said Jason. "But basketball's even better. Four quarters of watching guys run up and down the court? Mostly *down* the court. And those shorts? It's the whole package. But that's not just it. The NBA has some of the best butts in sports. Shit, check out Isaiah Rider. If that's not good ass, then what is?"

"I've never really noticed. Seriously." Ruben took a swig of his drink. "I think you and me are watching two totally dif-ferent games. They actually play ball in the game I watch."

"Yeah, they play ball in the one I'm watching, too,"

chuckled Jason. "It's definitely a spectator sport though."

Ruben pointed at the poster of Brian Grant, the tall, light-skinned brother with short, sexy dreadlocks. "What about him?"

"Oh, now Brian has some serious ass," said Jason. "But then you're gonna get that playing so much sport. Hell, basketball's definitely the one for it."

"You really like your butts," said Ruben.

"As much as you like basketball," said Jason, finally taking a sip of his drink. "If your posters and all are anything to go by."

"I don't think I'm as much of a connoisseur of my passion as you are," said Ruben. "You know, it took balls coming up to me like that."

Jason smiled, still in disbelief that he'd done that, that he was sitting on this stranger's couch, talking about butts. He had to put it down to the crazy, lazy sort of afternoon that it was.

"I don't come up to guys like that often," Jason said. "You got to believe me."

Ruben put the glass down. "Most guys I know who like guys—they more into dicks. I never met a guy crazy about ass."

"It's just like dicks, bro. Some big. Some thick. Ain't really no different from that."

"So what does it do for you? I don't see it."

Jason felt a little more of his single-minded courage. "Stand up."

"What?"

"Stand up." Jason motioned for Ruben to get up.

Unsure of Jason's intentions, Ruben rose hesitantly. Jason set his glass down, barely able to stop himself from busting out with a big ole grin.

"Put your hands on your ass," he said. Ruben paused, then complied. "Yeah, just like that. Now. Feel that?"

"Feel what?"

"*That.* That's what it is, bro. I can't even explain it. But what *that* is—what you're feeling in your hands right now—that's what I like about butts. That full, hard, smooth feeling. The shape. The look. It's where a guy's body starts. Everything else moves out from there."

Ruben hastily sat back down. Jason whined, jokingly showing his displeasure at Ruben giving up so readily.

"You know, I'd give anything to be on my back under your ass," Jason said.

Ruben laughed. "You serious, ain't you? I can tell."

"Fuck, yeah, I'm serious. You better believe it. For me, that's heaven. Right there. And your sorry butt is sitting on it, rather than feeling it like I told you."

Ruben smiled and Jason was quick to seize what already seemed like a perfect dream thus far:

"I'll give you twenty bucks to feel your butt."

"What?" Ruben looked a little put-out, but still smiled.

"You heard me, bro. Twenty bucks. All I want to do is feel it over." Jason felt himself almost beginning to pant. There was no way he wanted to leave here, after getting this far, without copping a feel of Ruben's rump.

"Just feel it? You serious?"

"Straight serious. Twenty bucks."

Ruben considered it, then laughed it off like it was some stupid high school dare. Then he paused, and finally answered:

"Tell you what: I'll let you feel it for free. I don't want to take your money. Not over something like feeling someone's butt."

"You don't know how much this means to me, bro. I swear, I don't see asses as good as yours every day."

"If you did, you'd be one very broke ass brutha." Ruben stood up, anticipating Jason's need to see the goods.

Jason sat there, not believing his luck, fearing one wrong word or move and life would revert back to what it had been before he came up here: Ruben just some stranger and Jason just some kid riding on his bike out on the street. But here he was, in some unbelievable turn of events, up in Ruben's pad. With a butt as good as his. And he didn't even want to take money to let Jason feel it up.

"Ok, what do you want me to do?" Ruben asked.

"Ah . . . just turn around."

Ruben rotated slowly as Jason reclined back on the couch and spread his legs a little, unable to help himself as his manhood began to harden within his baggy shorts. His eyes were locked on Ruben's rear end, taking in every smooth inch of those black shorts where they hung over his ass, smoothly contouring down, hinting at the one thing Jason wanted so badly.

"Pull your shirt up a little," Jason said. "It's sorta blocking the view."

Ruben's sleeveless T-shirt hit the floor beside him. Jason signaled him over a little closer, spreading his own legs wider, pulling his shorts tightly over his erection. He inched his hands forward as Ruben placed himself between Jason's knees.

Then Jason heard:

"Do what you want. It's all yours for the next ten minutes. I won't complain. I won't look, neither."

He grasped Ruben's tight globes, thrilling in the sensation of both the soft material of his shorts and the hard ass below. This was heaven. And this Rican was more than an angel. Jason was fully consumed in what stood before him. Fantasies rushed into his mind. He felt the hardness beneath his hands, causing greater hardness between his legs. He leaned forward and gently pushed his face against Ruben's butt.

Jason moaned quietly, his hands kneading Ruben's ass, sending his senses deeper into bliss . . . the firmness and fullness that he felt against his face . . . the softness of the shorts. Ruben pushed back against his face. Jason groaned. As if Ruben knew his every intimate want. With a desperate roughness, Jason removed his raid vest from his upper body, dumping it hastily. Then he unzipped his shorts and let his hand slip inside and scoop up his erection. He did this with his left hand while his right hand grappled with another obstruction: Ruben's shorts.

"You want me to pull them down a little?" Ruben asked.

"Yeah . . . but slow, ok?"

"Sure."

Jason took a moment to marvel over the strength in Ruben's back, the smooth curves inevitably leading downward. His eyes then moved to the waistband of Ruben's shorts and he gently put his hands on the warm skin just above Ruben's waist.

Everything led there eventually.

The waistband began creeping downward. The pace was almost painfully slow. *Was this guy a professional strip tease?* Ruben's thumbs were on either side of his waist, pulling down the shorts, revealing each smooth, tantalizing inch of his ass. Those shorts heralded the symphonies that lay blow. And Jason saw proof positive that the downward slope of Ruben's back helped form the beautiful fullness of his ass.

Jason moaned. Jacking. Staring. Ruben bent forward as he let his shorts fall. The final curtain down. Away from the main act. Perfection. Two thick, brown globes of hard muscle, parting ever so slowly. The tantalizing conclusion of his strong body. Jason cussed out loud, saying "damn" and "fuck" over and over as he saw more and more of Ruben's crack . . . the hint of tight black curls that peppered the smooth brownness . . . the heavy orbs of Ruben's nuts peeking out between his legs.

This is a dream. This is heaven and I'm dreaming.
Never wake me up.

He brought himself to his senses enough to lower his hand, hearing a quiet moan as his fingers roamed over the hardness of Ruben's ass. He let his thumb trace down the furrow of his crack, touching the gentle softness of his puckering hole . . . the way it filled his hand . . . the slight patch of hair there.

He pressed his face against Ruben's ass. The Rican push back and spread his legs, opening his cheeks up to Jason. The warmth against Jason's skin thrilled him, causing an erotic pleasure unleashed in his groin. He used his face as he would a hand, stroking Ruben's cheek with his cheek. His tongue pecked at Ruben's crack. His breath came as heated panting against the Rican's body. He could barely hear the sounds of his slurps matching the sounds of his hand on his own cock.

His nose and mouth pushed farther into the slightly hairy crack of the Rican's ass. The smell was intoxicating, the softness enhanced by sweat from the heat of the afternoon. Jason let his tongue wander, as his spare hand explored Ruben's body. Eventually, Jason unhanded his own penis to more fully grab the tight globes covering his face. From Ruben, he heard powerful moans like new sounds of nature in the warmth of a new summer. His tongue pushed mercilessly, his hands working, stroking, kneading. He found himself caught up in a high, pushing himself further and further upward. Pushing Ruben forward onto the floor. He wanted this ass firmly on the ground before him. He wanted to feel the hard resistance against his palms.

He found himself leading the Rican to one of the kitchen chairs and getting him to bend over it. Fixated on his lust and passion, Jason pushed his penis into the crack of Ruben's ass—not straight in, but up. It was a perfect match, key in lock. Sharing heat and intimacy.

As many times as he'd been with a guy, Jason had almost never done more than this against his partner's ass. Why would you want more? The pleasure of feeling Ruben's long furrow against his dick was more than enough. He thrilled at his lighter skin against Ruben's smooth brown flesh, his eyes and hands only now just seeing the beauty of the rest of the Rican's muscular body.

Thrusting, grunting . . . the sweat within Ruben's ass was more than up to the task of lubrication. Jason groaned powerfully, feeling his peaks swelling all too quickly . . . his jersey hanging off his own lanky frame . . . Ruben before him, naked . . . willing . . . open to the powerful thrusts along his crack. Jason cried out, both hands locked tightly on the orbs of Ruben's thick ass. His cock was ablaze with pleasure as he thrust and stroked.

Don't let this dream stop. It feels too good.

And then there was the pleasure in his raging, pulsing cock.

Jason grunted, all but yelled as his cum erupted. He pulled back, his first shot shooting directly against Ruben's asshole, then his crack. The Rican was also moaning, shooting his own load on the chair he was bent over. Jason thrilled at the sight of his thick, hot cum, white against Ruben's

smooth brown skin. His cock pulsated back and forth, rain-
ing sweet white globes of cum across the thick expanse of
beautiful butt. He bucked up hard and spurted out one last
shower of climax, yelping as suddenly, he felt his foot slip on
the rug and the rug slide across the floor.

Bam!

Already dizzied by the stars in his head from cumming, Jason felt new stars dancing within him. He was flat on
his back, staring up blankly. Smiling foolishly. Realizing how
stupidly eager he'd been. How his last thrust had sent him
tumbling backwards. He giggled as he thought about how
often he'd asked to be where he was now: watching that
smooth, beautiful Puerto Rican ass right above his head.

A few moments later, he realized that his pleasure was
more an aching pain. He could feel it in his back and head.
With a slight start, Jason realized that the Rican's ass was now
covered by the soft black material of his basketball shorts.
Jason also realized that he himself was dressed. The warm
heat seemed to be coming more from the world around him
than his groin. He put his hand up to his head, grimacing.

"Yo! Up here!"

Jason glanced up, the foliage of the trees above sheltering him somewhat from the sun's light. The Rican was
looking down on him. He had been the source of that rough,
heavy voice that sounded nothing like Jason had expected.
Jason groaned as he saw that his bike was lying beside him.
And that he was lying on the hard concrete of the road.

The realization came slowly.

"Fucking fool!" said the Rican. "You ran into the back of a parked car. What the fuck was you looking at that you didn't have your eyes on the road?"

Jason grinned sheepishly at the hard face staring back down at him.

Did he have to say?

Redhawk

Robinman

Redhawk's gloved fist arched upward in a powerful uppercut, laying the smuggler out cold with one powerful blow. The masked man then spun and gave the next attacker a right cross to the jaw, followed by a left hook that put the man out for the count. Redhawk looked back over his shoulder as he heard a soft "ugh" from his partner.

Bluejay rocked back a bit, the boy sidekick slightly stunned from the crowbar he'd taken across the back. The youth recovered and his muscular leg snapped out in a powerful side kick, hitting the smuggler in the stomach. At the same time, the boy's gloved fist smashed into the nose of the man in front of him. Blood spattered and the man went down in a heap. The teen whipped around, his cape twirling in the cold night air, his boot arcing around in a whistling circle-kick that intersected the man's jaw. The last smuggler collapsed in a heap and Bluejay grinned. Two on one wasn't a problem for the athletic lad. He looked over at Redhawk, the caped man already stepping over toward him.

Redhawk, AKA Marcus Solomon, financier extraordinaire, stood a full head taller than his teenaged partner. A hooded mask shaped like a great red hawk's head concealed the man's features, the rest of the skintight full-body costume being the color of dried blood. His trunks, gloves, boots and wing-like cape were all a darker red. He was a powerfully built man, with muscles like thick cables and a deep, strong chest. He glowered at the assembled criminals, all either unconscious or in so much pain that there was little chance of anymore fighting These men had been terrorizing the docks of Centropolis for months—advance men for a new Chinese syndicate trying to set up a presence in town. Redhawk nodded and put his hand on Bluejay's shoulder and gave his partner a gentle squeeze.

"Good work, son," Redhawk said. "A good eighteenth birthday present."

Bluejay nodded, a slight smile on the boy's full lips. Faint praise from anyone else, but from Redhawk, it was amazing. Bluejay had followed all the leads, finally finding out where the new gang was located. It was his work that allowed the crime-fighting pair to nab the criminals tonight. The boy's leather glove creaked as he made a fist. Bluejay, secretly freshman college student Ricky Dane, was built more along lithe acrobatic lines than his mentor. His costume was a medium blue bodysuit with dark blue trunks, gloves, boots and cape, though his cape was shorter—about the length of a poncho. His mask, too, was different: just a simple blue eye-mask that concealed the area of his face around his corn-flower-blue eyes. The youth grinned and ran fingers through his short golden hair.

"Thanks, partner," he said, then cocked his head. "The cops are on their way. We'd better be going."

"Right, son," the big man said and took a small device from his belt. He shot a line high into the air. The eagle-claw-styled grapple clamped shut on a building ledge and power-ful micro-motors drew the large man into the sky. Bluejay did the same and the pair left the scene as they had arrived.

Bluejay undid the cape and let it fall, then took off his gloves. He peeled off the mask, revealing the young, pretty features that made Redhawk's heart race. So beautiful! The boy was so beautiful. Eighteen years old, right in the full flower of his youth, Bluejay was poised on the brink of becoming a man. His body had strengthened and firmed, but still retained the suppleness and smoothness of a boy. He pulled off the skintight tunic, showing the deep chest and washboard-flat six-pack abdominals. The soft brown circles on the boy's pecs were raised slightly, the cold of the underground lab making the boy's nipples grow slowly erect. Soon they were pointed little brown nubs, hard and sensitive.

Redhawk watched his boy partner turn away, and his dark eyes drifted down Ricky's taunt, sleek body. Excellently

muscled, the boy looked like a perfectly proportioned Greek
statue. Each muscle flowed smoothly into the other. His arms
were hard and his shoulders broad. His back tapered down
. . . there. Redhawk smiled. Ricky's ass . . . it always amazed
him. How perfect it was, how smooth and sexy. Dimpled and
firm, the smooth white mounds were like sculpted marble.
The boy bent for something and Redhawk bit his lip, watching the smooth muscles flex and spread. The boy stayed in
that position, the youth's perfect ass framed and defined by
the skintight trunks he wore. They separated the hard globes
of his ass a bit, following the firm curves deep into Bluejay's
secret places.

Redhawk shifted where he stood, feeling the hot hard
length of his thick manhood move in his own trunks.
Bluejay. Ricky. His partner, friend, confidante. He licked his
lips and hungrily watched the youth, imagining how the boy
would feel under him, how his smooth sleek body would
respond to his touch. The man turned away so the boy would
not see his arousal and put his hands palms-flat on a work-
bench. A man could only take so much.

He felt Bluejay's touch on his shoulder and shivered.
"Is there something wrong, Redhawk? Marcus?" The boy's
voice was soft and concerned. Redhawk turned around. His
bulging trunks slid over Bluejay's, the soft skintight fabric
hiding nothing. His erection, thrust down his leg, pressed
into the boy's bare midriff like a red-hot brand.

"Yes," he breathed. "Something's wrong. I'm sorry,
Bluejay."

Ricky stared down at the bulge pressed against his baby-smooth stomach. He could see the length of the shaft and the flare of the man's cock crown. He'd seen Redhawk naked before, but it had never seemed so large. The man had a large cock, much larger than Ricky's member. Now, feeling it against him like this . . . he moved a bit, and Redhawk gasped as the boy's body slid across the hardness. Ricky moved back and then looked up into the boy's innocent blue eyes, so wide with amazement and . . .

Anticipation?

"Gosh, Redhawk. Did I cause that?" the boy whispered, his soft full lips barely parting. Redhawk put his hands on the boy's bare shoulders and squeezed firmly. Bluejay closed his eyes and kept his head tilted up, those soft red lips still parted just a bit.

A man could only take so much.

Redhawk bent and kissed the boy who had been like a son to him all these years. The boy's lips were soft and dewy, just like Marcus had always imagined. Ricky didn't resist him, didn't pull back, but instead moved into the kiss, kissing him back with a tender passion that surprised Marcus. His grip on Ricky's bare shoulders grew stronger. Bluejay slid his arms around Redhawk's deep chest and settled against the powerfully-built man.

The golden-blond boy drew back slightly, his wet lips kissing cheek and chin. "I like it, Marcus," the boy whispered. The youth moved his firm stomach muscles against Redhawk's erect cock and the man swallowed hard. "I didn't

know I caused you to get hard like that. I like the way it feels."
Bluejay dropped his hand to the man's trunks. His gentle
gloved fingers teased the shaft, tracing the bulge the crown
made. "You're really big, Redhawk. Can . . . can I see it?" the
boy whispered breathlessly.

Redhawk undid his belt and found the secret flap in
his trunks. A second later, the red, erect rod of his mancock
pushed out into the open air, springing erect in one swift
motion. It surged against Ricky's stomach, the flesh hot and
smooth.

"Oooooh!" gasped Bluejay. The masked boy went to
his knees. A gloved hand wrapped around the shaft. The
other hand slid over the massive purple crown, stroking it.
Redhawk shivered and pulled away from the teenaged boy,
stepping back. Ricky got to his feet and bowed his head.

"I'm sorry, Marcus, I . . . I thought . . ." The boy looked
up, tears running down his cheeks, soaking the blue mask he
wore. "I thought you wanted . . ."

"I want you," the masked man said and drew the boy
into his arms again, kissing the youth. Ricky relaxed against
him again, and now Redhawk could feel his boy-partner's
dick against his leg. He moved his leg against Ricky's erection
and laughed softly at the gasp of pleasure and need he wrung
from the boy. He moved his leg against the lad's trunks, then
slid his hand down to cup the teenager's manhood. He
manipulated the boy though his costume, then undid the
kid's belt.

He knelt and slowly undressed Bluejay, slipping off

Then Redhawk rolled the boy over on his stomach, and his gloved hand fell on the smooth perfect globes of the boy's ass.

Ricky's ass, his sweet perfect ass, was his at long last.

He pulled the drenched tights from the boy, then pulled off his own gloves. His hand slid up Ricky's bare leg, then gently over the firm full mounds that had fascinated him since the boy had started becoming a man. He felt the firmness, the supple strength, the baby-smooth white skin. He massaged the kid's firm ass, tracing the dimples in it, then his fingers dipped lower, deeper.

Marcus slid his fingers against Ricky's firm mounds, then between them, gently and teasingly tracing the boy's ass-crack all the way down to the place where the boy's balls attached. He slid his hand under Ricky's body, feeling the kid's cock and balls. He squeezed and massaged the boy's cock, which was already growing hard again.

Redhawk had to chuckle. The resilience of youth. . . .

Now the man returned his attentions to the full perfect globes before him, and bent over. He kissed each hard mound, his lips sliding over the baby-smooth skin like it was marble. "Oh, my perfect little boy," he sighed, and then he pulled the firm mounds apart, revealing Bluejay's most secret place, the softly quivering star-shaped hole: the object of the man's desire.

Redhawk slid his fingers gently over Bluejay's soft skin, tracing the firm ovals set before him. He felt his own cock grow painfully rigid in his tights and shifted slightly to

parted on their own. "Take me, Marcus, please? Do . . . any-thing you want with me." The kid breathed, his eyes closed in the depths of his passion.

Marcus Solomon, wealthy beyond counting, hand-some and athletic, able to have anyone he wanted in the world . . . wanted nothing more than the pretty young col-lege boy spread before him, the laughing, acrobatic lad he'd shared a world of dangers with. He bent forward now and kissed the twitching little hole, kissed and licked and kissed again. His tongue pressed the boy's gates open and suddenly he was inside, licking his kid-partner's ass! "Ooohh!" Ricky sighed, groaning like a Centropolis Square whoreboy.

Redhawk's powerful hands squeezed the boy's firm ass-cheeks, pulling the dimpled mounds apart so he could taste the boy's fruits. His tongue and lips were busy until Ricky gasped and all resistance crumbled. He let the boy down gently, then slid two fingers into the boy's ass. Bluejay writhed on the mat, feeling the thick digits invade his most private place. He twisted and groaned, his own cock trapped beneath the weight of his lean athletic form.

"Oh, God, Redhawk! Dude, that feels good."

Redhawk slipped his slickened fingers deeper and watched his boy twist on the mat and gasp and shiver with pain and delight. He plunged his fingers into the kid over and over, firmly yet gently, loosening the boy's ass, which clenched his digits so tightly.

Eventually Redhawk slipped his fingers out of Bluejay and stood up in order to strip off the rest of his costume. The denial had almost driven him mad with need, but now, his thick, ten-inch erection arched up into the air, finally free. He wrapped his hand around the shaft and felt his cock twitch. A soft pearl of pre-cum slid from the large red head and moved down the shaft before dripping down onto Ricky's buttocks.

Marcus knelt between his golden boy's thighs and caressed the kid's ass again, feeling the taut perfection. He pulled the globes apart and gently laid his shaft between the firm mounds.

Ricky gasped at the heat. "Is . . . is that your dick, Redhawk?" the boy asked, his voice a trembling whisper. The youth moved his hips, causing his ass to caress Marcus's cock. "Are you gonna fuck me?"

Redhawk pressed the shaft against Ricky, his body weight pressing the eighteen-year-old boy into the mat. Ricky groaned a bit. His rock-hard kid-dick was still trapped, and it was painful. Pleasure and pain. The boy wanted nothing else. He moved his ass again, clenching it so the firm mounds grabbed and held the hard shaft between them. The masked boy grinned when he heard the hiss of desire from his mentor, the man who had been like a father to him for so many years.

"I'm going to make love to you, yes. You are so pretty, Ricky, so very pretty. My beautiful little boy. Your ass is so perfect . . . I want it, Ricky, do you understand, son? I need you."

"Please, Redhawk, please take me. Marcus, take me,"

the kid moaned. Marcus took hold of his thick shaft and pressed the hard, plum-sized crown against Ricky's twitching anus. Then he pushed.

"Aaagghh!" Bluejay cried in a soft, high voice as the thick member invaded his tender virgin anus. "Take it out!" the boy pleaded.

Redhawk pushed the boy to the mat and slipped his cock farther inside. The boy was tight. God, was he tight. But now, he was opening up. Redhawk plunged his thick member all the way into the struggling kid's ass. Ricky's protests quieted, then died down. The boy's moans became moans of pleasure as Redhawk found his partner's prostate and began slowly and gently teasing it. He moved inside Ricky, his strong body pressing the handsome teen into the exercise mat, his cock diving deep into the boy's tight ass, deeper and deeper until he could go no farther. He plunged in and out, gasping at the heat and tightness until he felt his pre-cum gently squirt into the pretty lad's depths.

Time to slow down.

Redhawk pulled out. His penis stood upright, glistening with the spit he'd licked into Ricky's ass. The boy beneath him moaned and spread his muscled legs. Redhawk chuckled and slid his hand over the hard mounds, then slipped a finger into the boy's hole. Bluejay pushed back, eager to take the teasing digit.

"Gosh, Marcus, that was great!" said the kid.

"I'm not done yet, son," Redhawk answered. He turned the smiling boy over and slid his hand up Bluejay's

ing from the fuck and his own orgasm. Marcus bent and licked the sweet boy-cum from Ricky's chest, teasing the teen's nipples to hardness in the process. He bit them gently, then moved to the boy's neck and throat.

Ricky embraced him and Marcus settled his weight on the youth. He felt Ricky's still-twitching cock slide against his stomach as he kissed the beautiful young man. The boy returned the kiss eagerly, the heretofore virgin youth's enthusiasm more than making up for what he lacked in restraint or technique. The youth's hands glided over Marcus's magnificent body until they cupped the man's ass, his long slender fingers probing him and testing him.

Marcus grinned and pulled the boy's hands away, parting from his pretty partner, then helping the boy to his feet. Ricky embraced him and leaned against him, exhausted from his first fuck. Marcus held Ricky against his chest, smoothing the boy's hair back down. Then he tilted Ricky's face upward and kissed him again.

"Not now, my beautiful boy. Let's get you cleaned up. It's time for our night patrol."

"Awww, Redhawk!"

Redhawk grinned at the kid. "Afterwards. I promise."

With that, the masked boy smiled, gave the man a quick kiss and headed for the showers. Marcus followed after, looking forward to the boy dropping the soap as he always did.

Alabaster Ass

Jay Starre

I love ass, and this particular one was a prime example of all I love about it. I call it the Alabaster Ass. It was gorgeous beyond compare.

I had noticed the guy in the gym and at the pool for several weeks before I made my move. We had nodded and smiled. Our eyes had met and the flicker of interest that sparked was mutual and unmistakable. But I was in no hurry this time to scoop up my prey. Just watching Aaron move around was a turn-on in and of itself.

He was cute as hell, with short reddish-blonde hair, a square jaw, bowed lips and the lightest blue eyes, which were practically colourless. He smiled openly, which lent him a sexy yet innocent air that I found exciting. I wanted to make him moan and beg for it.

I wanted Aaron to beg for me to do his ass. That was

the thing about him, not just his good looks and sexy smile. He had the can from heaven. In a swimsuit, tight trunks hugged his two hard mounds like they were glued right on. I actually gasped out loud the first time I saw him at the pool. He was sprawled out on the outdoor deck, sunbathing in that skimpy suit. I sat close and watched him for a good hour while he soaked up the afternoon rays. Every once in a while he would roll his hips, or raise them up, offering me a different view of the twin peaks of perfection that were his butt-cheeks.

I was hooked from that moment. When I saw him in the gym the next day, I nodded and from his return smile, I knew it was only a matter of time. Why didn't I rush right in for the kill? The truth was, his ass was so damn perfect, I wanted to savour, for just a little while at least, the delicious thought of feeling it between my greedy palms.

My limit was about two weeks, reached when he changed in front of me in the locker room. That day I had nodded and said hello, and a few minutes later, he followed me into the locker room. He stripped directly across from me while I watched. He faced away from me as he tore off his sweaty tank top, revealing a hard, muscled back and a trim waist. Then he shoved down his gym shorts and jock strap, bending over as he did. I just about keeled over. What an ass! His back was very tan, but his butt was pure white, alabaster white. It was practically glowing neon in stark contrast to the darkness of his back and thighs where the summer sun had browned his skin.

He raised one foot to the bench in front of him to untie his shoes. He had taken his shorts off before his sneakers. I was treated to the sight of that ass spread open and parted as he unlaced one shoe, then the other. Big, hard and pristine white without a shred of hair I could note; it was, without question, perfect.

He turned as my eyes were fastened to that beautiful image, catching me in the act of blatant butt-surveying. I grinned and feebly attempted to hide my stiff boner, which was jutting out beneath my flimsy workout shorts.

"My name's Jay," I blurted out. "Want to come to my place for a beer?"

"Sure. I'm Aaron by the way." He grinned at me, his own dick beginning to grow as he hastily wrapped a towel around himself.

He showered while I dressed, afraid to follow him and display my raging boner to the rest of the locker room. We left together and walked to my place a few blocks away. Once inside, we were in each other's arms seconds after closing the door.

Sloppy, wet kisses and duelling tongues made for a good start. I groped his hard butt, reaching behind him and placing a hand on either cheek and squeezing, pulling him close against me. That ass felt awesome, hard but hefty, some real meat on there, not some little tight ass without any substance. I was shoving my stiff cock into his stomach and gripping his butt like there was no tomorrow when he broke the embrace and gasped out the words I was praying to hear.

"Do my ass, I know you want it. You've had your eyes on it for the past two weeks and been driving me nuts with all the waiting."

"Don't you worry!" I choked out, my mouth watering, my hands ripping at the waist of his jeans. "Get naked and on your belly with your ass in the air," I added while trying to catch my breath.

He complied, tearing off his pants and underwear along with his shoes as he hopped around my living room on one foot and then the other. I was shedding my own clothing in record speed: T-shirt, jeans and shoes flying in every direction, my eyes fixed on the unveiling of his awesome body.

He had an athletic build: broad shoulders, slim waist, that rounded, hard can, bold thighs and powerful calves—a total package that fit together flawlessly. He did not disappoint. When he plopped down on the couch facedown with his thighs spread wide, my eyes moved to the area of my most intense fascination: his perfect ass.

I was stroking my hard-on and groaning as I approached him. There it was, naked and available on my own couch, that alabaster ass! I stood over Aaron, his head turned to the side so he could look up at me with those amazing eyes, staring at me with melting lust, willing me to move toward the object of my own overwhelming lust.

I knelt beside him, reaching out to touch his butt. When my eager hands connected with that butt, the two big mounds quivered, as if they had a life of their own, excited to have me touch them. We both moaned. I ran my fingers over each mound, delighting in their satiny warmth, their pristine, pale, alabaster whiteness, framed by tan lines so the whole butt was one amazing piece of artwork.

I ran my fingers along the rounded cheeks, slowly exploring the trembling flesh, moving in circles from top to bottom, moving close to the parted crack, that deep furrow that was not yet open enough to reveal the depths within. I teased his ass, stroking around in slow, sensuous circles while my dick bobbed at my waist and screamed for satisfaction. I ignored it, focussing on that alabaster ass and its wondrous beauty.

My fingers galvanized him. He began to raise his hips and move into my caresses, obviously wanting more. I smiled with pleasure, gripping each cheek more forcefully, pulling them apart and pushing them together, feeling the strength in each big ass muscle, staring down at the crack as it parted and closed so sensually.

"Spread it," I murmured, not looking at him, staring at his beautiful butt instead.

His wordless reply was to raise his thighs slightly and get on his knees, shoving them wider. That was enough to reveal his crack in its entirety. I gasped. My eyes zeroed in on a hairless furrow, with a small, crinkled opening right in the center, which was his smooth palpating asshole.

My fingers plunged in that offered crevice, moving together into it, sliding along the impossibly smooth skin, so smooth it was like polished ivory, so hairless it had to have been shaved that way. My cock surged at the thought of

Aaron shaving that crack, getting the razor in there, cleaning away any vestige of hair until it was slick as silk.

I tickled the crack for a few minutes, grazing the pulsing orifice in its center, smiling at Aaron's reaction, his ass heaving up into my fingers, wiggling and grinding as he moaned incoherently, begging without words for more.

Penetration was what he desired. Every time my fingers crossed that wrinkled slot, it pulsed and twitched, parting slightly. I finally settled on it, teasing the opening with light caresses, grinning as he huffed and gyrated on the couch. Finally I did what I had wanted to do since I first laid eyes on that ass. I dropped my head and buried my face in the spread crack. I inhaled clean ass scent as my nostrils grazed his ass-flesh. I opened my mouth and stuck out my tongue, swiping down his crack until I fixed on his pulsing asshole. I tongued the tiny slot, tickling it as Aaron let out encouraging groans and shoved his ass in the air to meet me.

I tongued the entrance, licking the rim that expanded and gaped apart for my edification. I used both hands and pulled his butt-cheeks apart, then got my fingers right beside that snug hole and pulled it apart as well. I shoved my tongue deep, feeling the satiny warm inner flesh.

"Oh, gawd! Your tongue is up my ass!" Aaron blurted out.

My tongue rimmed his inner sanctum like it was a Thanksgiving feast. I muttered something, a garbled urging to spread his legs wider.

Miraculously he understood.

He rose right up on his knees, his face buried in the pillows, his ass in the air. I followed with my tongue buried in his ass-slot, stabbing as deeply as I could. He was a moaning mess, writhing and humping backwards, loving every second of it.

I lifted my face from his butt and stared down at it. The cheeks were flushed pink by then, his lust rushing blood to the sensitive area. His balls dangled down between his spread thighs, two round lemons of manly flesh. His crack was wet with spit, glistening and trembling. His little butt-hole was tremulous with desire, snapping open and shut as he groaned with his face in the couch pillows. I groaned myself as I pulled his cheeks wider with one hand and rammed the fingers of the other right into the center of that wet hole.

"Aggghh!" he blubbered into the pillows.

Two of my fingers were buried to the knuckle. The spongy orifice parted to oblige me, then snapped shut around my fingers. I shoved them deeper, stretching him open, grinning lustily at his antics as he shoved his butt backwards to impale himself on even more of the twin invaders. He was shouting out his protests, but his body was betraying him. Abruptly his asshole gaped wide open and my fingers slid in to the hilt, several inches of flesh embedded in his quivering slot.

"Fuck me!" He lifted his face and hissed at me, his lips wet with drool, his colorless eyes wild with desire.

He was hot and I went a little crazy. I fucked him with

those two fingers, lifting his alabaster ass right up off the couch with forceful thrusts, squeezing his ass-cheeks with my other hand and digging into his guts with all my might. He took it with huffing gasps, throwing his thighs wider and even reaching down between his legs and gripping his own hard dick and beginning to flail at it with the power of his excitement. I took one of his hands and placed it on my own stiff whanger, so that he was jerking his cock with his left hand and mine with his right.

I shoved my fingers way up inside him, feeling the tightness of his anal walls, and the cavern beyond where I was poking at his sensitive prostate and eliciting moaning little sighs out of him at the same time. I twisted them as I pummelled him, delighted with the way his hefty butt jiggled and quivered with each deep penetration.

I was ready to fuck him good with my stiff cock. Just thinking of it had me leaping up and fumbling on the coffee table for the conveniently located bottle of lube. In seconds I was squirting his writhing buns with a copious supply of the translucent gel, amazed at how sexy it looked glistening over his white butt and flushed crack. The stuff drooled down his ass-crevice and pooled in the gaping center of his twitching slot.

I crawled up between his legs and pointed my aching cock right at it.

"Go for it, fuck me with your big meat! Fill me up with cock! Fuck my ass!" Aaron encouraged me, waving his ass in front of me.

I didn't need any more of an invitation than that to get me going. I held his butt with both hands and shoved. The slippery opening parted like the Red Sea for Moses, gaping apart and swallowing me whole. My cock sunk right to the balls in his heated, palpating asshole.

"Oh man, oh fuck, oh gawd, I'm in your sweet ass," I whimpered, so excited I almost shot right then.

It was heaven in there. His asshole opened up for me, yet was still a massaging tunnel of warm flesh. Aaron wasn't content to just take my cock; he fucked himself with it. He was humping my meat with abandon within seconds of that first impalement, writhing all over the couch and caterwauling loudly like a slut in heat.

I stared down at that amazing ass, spread wide for my cock, the purple shaft ramming in and out of the white flesh, fat and huge, disappearing into the depths then reappearing as Aaron writhed and pumped and shouted. It was awesome. His asshole sucked me right to the limit, gripping my cock and then releasing it in steady pulses as Aaron expertly milked me to an incredible explosion.

"I'm cumming! I'm shooting right up your hot ass!" I screamed.

"Fill me with your jizz! Fill me up!" he shouted back, humping his sweet ass all over my spraying dick.

I was helpless in his grip. My cock erupted, my balls emptied and I collapsed on top of him, a sweaty, mindless quivering mass of flesh. I almost fainted as my heart pounded and my lungs laboured through my incredible orgasm.

Aaron went wild beneath me, working himself to an orgasm of his own with my hard cock spewing up his guts.

I felt his asshole snapping around my emptying cock as he too released his demons. Jizz sprayed beneath us onto my couch. I couldn't have cared less about that. The ripe stink of our sweat and cum permeated the air around us. I rode him to the end, sprawled over his jerking body until he too collapsed beneath me onto the couch.

We lay there for some time, our bodies quivering sporadically as our breathing stabilized and our heartbeats returned to normal. Finally I rose and pulled out of him. I stood up on quivery legs and surveyed him.

His head was turned to the side, those beautiful colourless eyes watching me, a lazy grin on his soft lips. His body was limp, totally relaxed as he lay on the couch without moving. I gazed at the width of his broad back, my eyes wandering down to his waist and then back to those amazing butt-cheeks. They were sweat-soaked and glistening with a sheen of lube. Although mostly alabaster white, there was a flush in the centre of each cheek, and in the crack. While I stared, Aaron sighed, and then he slowly spread his thighs and raised them.

I got a good look at his crack, lubed and just fucked. The spongy asshole was gaping open, stretched and hot and slick with grease and a trace of cum. I almost fainted again, weak at the knees at the sight. I wanted more, I was a slave to that incredible butt and that inviting asshole. I dropped to my knees and once more buried my face in it.

"Eat my just-fucked ass, go for it! Yeah, eat my ass and then fuck me good again! I know you want it, you want my ass more than anything in the world! Take it, take it again!"

With those words in the air, I descended to the depths.

He had me by the balls.

I surrendered to that alabaster ass.

And loved every moment of it.

Boo

Michael Skiff

Butt built by basketball
High and Mighty
Atop a pair of long-legged Wrangler
And high tops
He was the Converse Cowboy

We cruised in the arcade
And talked in the lot
Of Zorba's adult bookstore
On a warm, desert spring night
I followed him to his place

Recent rental expansion in Phoenix
Afforded Boo a quality crib
Furnished with a mattress,
A TV, a bike
And a basketball

His naked, black thighs
Went over my white shoulders
Schooling Boo's booty
In the safe stuff
Though we would become dropouts

Together we freaked
His ass like pussy
Pulled me inside
And without touching himself
He came

Kenny was from New York
where his people
Called him Boo
Just twenty-four years of age
In my city, he was new

That night, the dates
On our driver licenses
Sealed the bond
August 26
The day we both were born

A pari-mutuel teller by trade
A B-boy on the side
Boo was blessed with a smile
Like that other great player
Magic

We lived together
Several times
In several places
Once with his little girl
Visiting Daddy and his friend

We lived apart
Quick to anger
I feared his temper
Like the hammer
he once held to my head

I pressed
We should test
The results weren't the best
I passed, Boo's silence
told me all the rest

Back home
his peeps were clueless
When he began to slip away
He wouldn't tell them he had the funk
Let alone that he was gay

Sarasota in the summer
Martin Luther and Mahalia
Flapping the breeze
In front of our faces
At Boo's funeral

Someone donated
A loud, yellow Sunday coat
For his viewing
Did his people wonder
Why the white boy was here?

Magic had an announcement to make
But it was six months too late
To make a difference
For my Boo
To help him keep the faith

Laszlo's Bottom

Laszlo's Top Fan

Laszlo's bottom is milk-white and smooth of cheek. Part those cheeks and you find a thicket of curly, jet-black hair which almost succeeds in hiding the anal ring from view. This would be a pity, as it is not the virginal pinprick of an anus that you might expect between the lush cheeks of a virgin (amateur) footballer. The lips are fleshier, the crack lengthier, and though tight, more pliant than anticipated. His legs are, on the other hand, those of a footballer—not just the thighs, which gym workouts and sporting activity could render full and strong—but the calves as well. Maybe it is all that running after and kicking of the ball that make the calves so powerful. Yet, they in turn could not make the legs so hairy or the contrast between the pale smooth cheeks and the forested muscular legs so pronounced. He has been blessed by some god of polymorphous perversity.

But I am getting ahead of myself, many years ahead, as it happens. The power of the phrase "Laszlo's bottom" is not just in its referent: the astounding backside (astounding because its reality not only matches but surpasses the beauty once only imagined by this obsessive Laszlo fan). The phrase remains, ages after the first sighting of the real thing, a mantra that kept me stimulated when there was no chance for a wank at the expense, as I once put it, of Laszlo naked. Just saying the phrase brought me nearer to the goal of all my desires for those years of Laszlo-bottom-starvation. It reminded me that Laszlo had a bottom, that it was not just something dreamed up by a pervert's lust. Yet, it seemed so wonderfully perverted that he had one, granted by Nature, although the lust it inspired felt so defiantly unnatural.

So I'd say the phrase out loud, when I had the chance. "Laszlo's bottom" and then a pause, to contemplate it in imagination. That was the favourite, but there were many variants: "Laszlo's bare bottom" (possibly my favourite), "Laszlo's arse" (we are in the UK, after all and Britspeak for "ass" works so much more powerfully for me than "ass" could), "Laszlo's beautiful bum" (alliteration is so porno-graphic), "Laszlo's fanny" (now, that is Americanspeak, a word little kids used in the "arse" sense when I visited friends outside New York City), and, when fired by a Laszlo-wank, "Laszlo's cunt", "Laszlo's quim", "Laszlo's hole", "Laszlo's fuck-hole", "Laszlo's shithole". The last word would have had the same measure of unvarnished truth about it if uttered with any other bottom in mind. Yet, while I could imagine that Laszlo did have a bottom, I couldn't persuade myself that somebody as beautiful as he could shit or fart like other less obsessively worshipped mortals. Although, if he did, it did not detract one bit from its quality in my fever for his bot (yet another variant).

When I first set eyes on Laszlo, he was 20 and I was 39. Add on roughly two decades and you are only slightly ahead of where we are now in age. I have always loved arse. Any male as handsome would have had me checking out his jeans at the moment of his departure from my room. It is a tribute to Laszlo's face and a confession of my earliest obsession with it that I forgot for those first moments that he had an arse, let alone cock, balls, pubic hair, tits, pits. He turned out to possess all of these, but it took some years before I saw for myself. In the meantime, I kept forgetting even those vital areas.

Laszlo was my newly arrived student. He had not intended to study with me—*under me* sounds so facetious and forced. At the last minute of enrollment, he had requested a change from one of his two subjects to mine. He had not seen me. I had not seen him. The course was full, I had insisted on the telephone. The woman from whose subject he was changing came to see me to intercede for him. I said that I'd see him but was unlikely to change my mind. "He's very pretty," she added as she left after pleading his cause. This was less an insinuation about the relevance of this to my decision. Rather, it was something she had to confess that she'd noticed for herself, I felt. At her departure, I snorted to myself. Prettiness did not work for me.

It had been the wrong word. He was not pretty, but he was overpoweringly attractive. Less virile than he was to seem because he looked so young at that first moment, he still suggested an understated masculinity that grabbed my full attention. His look was friendly. There were smiles which allowed me to check out his teeth and even tongue. Because his eyes held mine, as they always did when we met, I did not have the chance to check out his body. His clothes did not accentuate it, in any case. I could hardly miss the fact that he was tall and strong-looking. He told me before I had learned his name that his father was Hungarian. I felt no surprise at this. The darkness of his hair and brown eyes told me he was not English by extraction, though his complexion was not swarthy. The film-star looks suggested more exotic origins than the prettiness and blondness of several of his peers. I was captivated. I dared on that first meeting to hope that he was too. He was not, at that moment, but I judged by the parting look and smile.

Later, I was irritated that I had not examined his retreating view more painstakingly. That was putting it mildly. I had hardly any impression of what was definitely my favourite portion of male anatomy, so potent was the face spell. I wanted his arse to be full and firm and fuckable, but even those terms felt out of place as never before. So it was true. Even dirty old men (I'm dirtier and older now, of course, but I knew what I was going to be back then) can fall in love—and with a face.

It didn't take long for me to see that there is no fool like a (dirty) old fool. Only days afterwards, I saw him at a table in the canteen gazing adoringly at a dusky, slim female student. She gazed back with the confident smile that anybody would feel to have inspired him. His adoration mocked mine. It was the same look I was trying now not to be caught directing at him. When he saw me, he smiled and waved. If he felt for me even an iota of what I did for him, he'd have been less cheerful and spontaneous, I knew. His uncomplicated masculinity—the understatement of it making it so much more credible—put me and my daft fantasy life in perspective. That's what it was. Fantasy. In one way, the realisation was merciful. It enabled me to control myself long enough to see that he had a body and would probably have an arse.

Perhaps it was that same understated masculinity that made him dress in clothes that were never baggy but never clung or exhibited him either. I would glance at his long legs in the jeans and at the way the seat of them covered him but did not tease the voyeur. Then I'd see his face and my stomach would lurch and I'd forget my search all over again.

There were so many times that he seemed almost within some sort of reach. He would find reasons to visit me in my office, usually late in the day when I was on my own. He would sometimes seek me out earlier in the day in the canteen to sit with me over coffee. But when he did, we talked of his studies or even of his girlfriend. The word "normal" insisted itself, even when academically and personally I made a point of spurning the category. At night, I would feel almost ashamed at what I put him through then. My wanking had always been wild and frequent, but frenetic as it was with Laszlo as the subject of my wank fantasy, I tried to keep scenarios possible (admittedly, not probable). I had no chance of touching, let alone sexually assaulting his bottom, bum, arse, fanny, cunt, fuckhole; but I would imagine him taking pity on me and allowing me to hire him as my personal private nude model. The poses would start subtly, but would graduate into bottom display, buttocks thrust out at the camera, cheeks held open for the lens to pry, legs back over head in the abandon of anal exhibitionism. I'd cum. Not all that much later, it would be morning and I'd realise on meeting him how foolish all this was. He was too friendly and unembarrassed for there to be any remote hope of sexual games to be played or even consented to.

When I did have the chance to linger over the details of his bottom, when he stood with his back to me once in charcoal gray trousers at a minor celebration, I felt disappointed. The material seemed to hang from his waist without much buttock impediment. Oh no. He was flat-arsed, undersized of cheek and probably scrawny where I had envisaged thrusting, quivering mounds. The handsomeness of his face and the sweetness of his personality would have to be enough, I decided. It was possible to be hopelessly in love with a man with no arse to speak of. That would have been out of the question before Laszlo, but whatever physical disappointment there might one day be, he was my idol. I could not see how that could change.

One of the warmer days, he suddenly pulled his sweater off in class. He had some trouble with getting it over his head. All my visual attention went to the forest of silky black hair at each armpit. I felt dizzy, stopping in the middle of an idea, trying to regain the momentum of my lecture so that every student eye would not follow my line of vision. As much as anything, I wanted this brazen pit display to be for me and nobody else but me. I could see that it was not. Yet, if he could flash his pit hair at me without a thought for what he was doing to me, I might be luckier eventually.

I was. Unbelievably lucky. One morning, I was ending my session with the unimpressively few weight machines in the gym balcony, with nobody else at all around, when I became aware of shower water running. Nobody else had been up to the balcony during my workout. Perhaps it was a homeless student grabbing some hot water and a quick wash. This did not excite me, because the shower curtains would be pulled together, and anyhow, he'd be finished by the time I reached the downstairs changing room, I reckoned.

No, it was Laszlo. You guessed anyhow, so why prolong the non-existent suspense? If it is no surprise to you, it was surprising beyond words to me. He had made no attempt to close the curtains. I felt my knees buckle when he looked up, naked and smiling, from his soap work on his body. Once he turned his eyes on me, I could never drop the look. I wanted to look at his body, but the urge was not so great that I could deny him the return of his gaze. I prayed that peripheral vision might be strong enough. I knew that his naked body was beautiful, but it was frontal beauty and I could just about deal with not seeing that clearly. Then he turned round. I felt so overwhelmed at the unexpectedness of his bare bottom that everything seemed to go into a blur. I longed for sharp focus, but all I could achieve was the soft variety. He continued to talk to me. It would have been rude to look anywhere but his naked back, but I could not register the details, maddening as the failure was even at the time. He chatted but left my mind—and my eyes—free to wander. While the detail kept eluding me, I could see that this arse was far more beautiful than my imagination at its most masturbatory could make it. The flesh was peerlessly smooth and white. Because it was also wet, it looked like some sort of statuary that rain was teeming down. How his bottom could look skinny in trousers baffled me. It turned out to be fleshy and voluptuous, but also sculpted in a way that suggested tightness and firmness at the same time.

And that was it for quite some time till after he had graduated. If this were a love story, I'd spend many pages telling the next part. It is, in a way, of course. I love both Laszlo and his bottom. But I can hear cries of "enough already, cut to the chase." They are coming from my own head as well as from imagined readers' mouths.

On the way swiftly to the chase, I will say that our friendship became franker when he no longer needed my teaching. He, who had never felt any queer desires till then, had been alarmed by his attraction to me, not on that first day, but the first time he saw me talk to his class. He'd not understood it, and still can't, he says. We tried bedding down together one Friday night at his place, but though I could hardly miss the fact that his cock was very stiff in the pajamas he insisted on wearing, it did not feel right to either of us. Still, we experimented.

He discovered next that he enjoyed being sucked off by a man. By me, to be precise. I had him naked while I blew him. My hands did caress his cheeks but I did not dare to play with his hole as I wanted to do. When my mouth filled with jets of his spunk, I savoured and swallowed them. He admitted later that he was shocked that I did not spit his cream out. This was well into the age of HIV consciousness, but he seemed to have led a surprisingly sheltered life even by het standards, I rationalised. But it would have been sacrilege to have spat out his cream and, yes, it was foolish, but I had to taste his spunk.

Another time, I did finger his hole while I sucked. He did nothing to stop me. There was no reciprocation from him, but I heard or felt no objections. The way he gave himself up to my ministrations and the blast from his cock each time I went for seduction were proof that this was not exactly hustler indifference from him. On my way home, I noticed that a tiny fleck of brown was lodged in my fingernail. This surprised me as Laszlo had affirmed once what I already knew—that he was almost pathologically clean and deodorised at just about any moment of the day. My guess is that the rare fleck of brown came from his not having a bidet (who does in Britain?) and not yet being used to the urgency of homosexual desire for his bottom hole. My finger smelled paradoxically clean with only the faintest whiff of heated hole.

I decided it was time for him to be rimmed. One evening, I had teased him into erection—big, very hairy cock and plump but not oversized ball-sac—when I got him to kneel above my head, with knees well parted so that I could place my head between them. I persuaded him to lower his body by licking the grooves between ball-bag and thigh, then lapped at his perianal ridge. By now, I had a heart-warmingly close view of his creamy buttocks. These were parted, so I could revel in the viewing of the tangle of dark curls that festooned his valley walls. I sniffed as close as I dared. The crack smelled freshly washed, as I expected it to. I let my tongue wander into his crack, where it had never been before, but then slipped the tip up to move along that most private slit in his holy of holies. He made no noise or sudden move, but stood his ground unflinchingly, as it were. I wanted to kiss and lick some more. I had not been encouraged but then had not been discouraged either.

It is a big mistake in some ways to fall in love with a lust object. You waste time wondering if he is doing you a favour repugnant to him and deciding whether or not to capitalise on what can only be his kindness. Even with my tongue lapping at Laslzo's arsehole lips, it never occurred to me that Laszlo not only had an anus but was highly anal. My education in the possible bentness of the apparently straight male was beginning in earnest. He confessed that he had always taken breaks from monogamy by retreating to the bathroom and sitting on the toilet masturbating to climax. He told me he liked to play with his ring and to augment his pleasure used the necks of plastic shampoo bottles to fuck himself with. These words were not his, mind you. The trouble is that I can't recall now just how he "confessed" these charming pastimes.

In early 1993, I bought a camcorder. Since then, many other males of all sorts of sexual persuasion have been probed and captured naked. Nevertheless, it was bought *for* him and remains primarily the means of celebrating and storing the beauty of his face, cock, chest, belly, legs, and above all, arse. What I began to realise on holiday with him during what was for him one exceedingly painful break-up from his girlfriend of the time, and before his disastrous marriage, was that Laszlo was a true exhibitionist. No mirror could be passed without a loving gaze into it, and he not only dressed for effect (yet always subtle) but showered and shaved for it, too.

He denied it at first but broke under my mockery. It was not conceit. He had not been fully aware of his charisma till I had spent years telling him of it. He'd hoped that he had it but had never been sure, because women, at whom it was first directed, never did respond in the frank way that I had. He began to enjoy the pleasure he was capable of giving me just by allowing me to study his face and body, and furthermore became conscious that there were good reasons why men stared at him in the street or in pubs and on tube trains.

He seemed frankly delighted to know he was queer-bait.

In my wildest fantasies, I never expected to find him such an easy nude model. That very first time, he posed with his full erection straight on, to the side, from above, from below, and offered me his arse in profile, in semi-profile, and then full on. He got on a chair to squat to an impossible depth, opening his cheeks so far that even the thick curls in his crack allowed unobstructed viewing of his capacious hole.

And it did look capacious. Tight and shiny, but at the same time welcoming—and all in all, more generous than you might expect a virgin hole to be. (Virgin hole it remains technically, untouched by cock, as Laszlo himself put it once. That leaves a lot for it to be touched by, admittedly.)

Laszlo cheerfully admitted that he used a finger to fuck himself with on some occasions and then there had been that business with the shampoo bottle necks. When I handed him his first vibrator and a tube of KY, he looked them over and over on camcorder as if they were sacred objects whose function in the present day he could not fathom. Eventually, it seemed that even his (feigned?) sweet innocence worked it out. He cocked one muscular leg, his cheeks parted visibly, a busy finger began anointing his hole till the surrounding hair was matted against the valley walls and he gingerly slipped the vibrator up his hole. Perhaps he was attempting modesty or maybe he genuinely felt alarm at the rubber cock now entering him. He went ultra slowly at first, but soon he had the vibrator all the way up to its base in a surprisingly rapid swallowing motion. "How do you switch it on?" he mumbled, not daring to meet my gaze. I left my place behind the lens and turned the base. It whirred into life. He wanked contentedly and used the fingers of his left hand to keep up a pleasant-looking fuck motion with the vibrator till he splattered his belly and tits with a copious load of spunk. I kept the camera running as he removed the vibrator, switched it off, inspected it (lubricated but notably clean), wiped it off on some tissues, wiped his own bumhole and left to wash in the bathroom.

His solos became more explicit in later camcorder sessions. I loved watching him finger himself to climax. It was a perfect act of precise and controlled anal masturbation, resulting in what seemed like a very satisfying and messy orgasm. It was exciting to be allowed to finger his cavern before he did so himself. His ring gave nicely and allowed me in to the moist warm velvet of his rectum. The prostate gland was easy to discover and to rub appreciatively. I noticed, with pleasure and a lot less of the lover guilt I once had known, that a turd was waiting some way higher than his prostate. While scat holds no appeal normally, the thought of him finding relief on the toilet was a pleasure to conceive.

I have had him brazenly piss into the toilet bowl or even into a glass jug for the camcorder's pervy delectation. So far, I have never had him shit—or "defecate" as one of his most lust-driven and kinky admirers loves to term it as he imagines the view—but I think it would not be beyond feasibility. I do get him to tell me, on holiday together when he disappears from the swimming pool area to the bathroom with the hotel room key, for example, what he does when he's in there. "Number twos," he often replies in a teasing performance of sweet childlikeness. I hope sometimes he will elaborate. He has, in fact, boasting of the regularity with which he shits in the morning and of the size and consistency of some turds, thanks to his healthy diet. This is rare, though. Generally, he does not go beyond the number involved.

I once thought that a man of his beauty would simply never fart. The absurdity of this was brought home on two occasions when he produced silent but deadly evidence that he can and does. Neither of us mentioned the events. Once though, he admitted that in every long-term relationship there is that difficult moment when a fart has to be acknowledged by one party or the other. I told him that I wanted to hear one from him one day or I'd not believe he was capable of farting (craftily suppressing the evidence I had already had). The very next day, he called out to me that I should listen carefully. He ended a torrential piss with a loud sharp report from between his bottom-cheeks. His broad grin after the fart was as boyish as any I have seen on his face.

But the deviance that we share goes well beyond that. Early in his posing career for me, I discovered that Laszlo has a more than natural affinity for nude exhibitions, and that his bottom is more wildly alluring than any fantasy could have prepared me for. I now wanted other men to have a chance to see him. I had the thrill of wildly tempting some by loans of his video footage. One masturbated to climax, groaning his name, in my front room while sharing a viewing with me. I told Laszlo later. He was pleased, more pleased than I dared to hope. I asked him if he'd provide this friend, a visiting American of no great beauty, with a show. He consented.

Bob, the American admirer, hired a room in a seedy gay hotel. Laszlo appeared looking very respectably be-suited after work. Bob spent a long time admiring the warmth from his hole, as he described it, caressing his bottom through his suit, but eventually stripping him naked and making him pull his knees to his chest to open up his arsehole to our eyes and eventually to his passionate kisses. Bob had Laszlo demonstrate how he fucks his wife (of that time) and Bob took pleasure in inserting his face between Laszlo's cheeks and tonguing him out while he did so. Laszlo seemed in his element, allowed to be queer without the responsibility of it.

The ideal way to build on this pleasure was to offer his services as a photographic model. He charged little money and was exposed to some ugly older men, but he enjoyed this aspect, especially if the customer allowed me to come along and camcord the details of his exhibition. Both of us got special pleasure if the "client" displayed a special fondness for his cheeks, crack, hole, and wanted to finger as well as rim him. The delight I felt to see my idol molested and invaded by other men was a genuine revelation to me. Yet, it was equaled by his own to have me watch. One of the most intense stares I have had from him was when I lay back on a hotel bed, clothed, looking up at him naked being sucked off and intermittently rimmed by a lustful, also clothed, client in his seventies. He had had a few drinks that evening and had admitted on the way that exhibitionism for me with a complete stranger, one who had no chance of "regular" sex with him, was one of the most profound sexual pleasures he had known. He seemed to love the humiliation aspect. He had told me that the idea that he was off limits to men but was suddenly made available by the laying down of a few banknotes excited him. It excited me, certainly. On that particular evening, he announced in mid-exhibition that the client would have to cease sucking long enough for him to go to the bathroom, but then added that we were welcome to accompany him. We knelt watching him spray the porcelain.

Laszlo now feels he is too mature and in too respectable a job to go on with his promiscuous exhibitionism. Before he reached this stage, he did however appear on the front cover and six full colour pages of a gay magazine, fully nude, but tragically never from the rear. He was even used as a model for a mobile phone, chatting amiably in just his black boxer shorts with a presumed boyfriend.

The days of bottom exhibitionism are not gone. He lives with his permanent girlfriend of the period, but still comes to see me so that we can go naked together into a "mixed" sauna where he loves to strut (he never wears his towel and only carries it in his hand). More importantly, he is exposed on several websites and laps up e-admiration from those who discover the wonders of his arse exhibitions.

Men recognise the allure of every part of him, from face to feet, and respond to his easy charm if he drops an e-mail in reply. The most intense enjoyment of him and for him relates always to his wondrous bottom. I am proud to have been and to remain the means of its exposure to the world.

Buns For Dessert

Beau Fesses

Belgian chocolate's great. Swiss chocolate's better. But ass-chocolate is the best of all.

I moved into the neighborhood a short six months ago to work for a public relations firm in the Manulife building. I'm what you call your standard, hopelessly yuppyish yuppie: suit and tie every day, nice, conservative, trim haircut, shoes carefully laced and shined, and a spiffy, alligator-leather briefcase. My big decision every morning is whether to wear a tie-clip or go wild and let my necktie flap freely in the wind. That's the most animalistic things get with me these days. Pretty pathetic, huh? Most of my colleagues have no idea I'm a homo-boy who craves butt constantly. And in vain. There's no action at all in the one-horse suburb where I live. At least not until last month when I discovered a quaint, little bakeshop around the corner. The window full of cream-topped meringues and strawberry-iced birthday tarts drew me in. I've always had a sweet tooth.

When I entered, a little bell above the door rang. Then I saw this guy, about 25, bent over beside the counter. I nearly dropped my brief case. He was leaning over a tray of cookies, his ass facing me—and what an ass it was! Two bulbous, firm, subtly rounded cheeks pressing against his white, thin-cotton baker's pants.

When he turned around, he said, "Good afternoon, sir." He had thick, red hair, a square, chiseled jaw, and a small, gold earring in one ear. No other guy around here had the guts to wear an earring.

He smiled at me, then lowered his eyes and smirked. I glanced down and saw my dick was tenting the front of my dress pants. Embarrassed, I placed my briefcase in front of my crotch, but the hard rectangular surface pressing into me only made my dick harder.

"May I help you, sir?"

I realized I hadn't looked at any of their desserts and stammered, "Ah, chocolate. I want chocolate."

"Chocolate?" He adjusted his paper baker's hat. "What do you mean, chocolate? Do you want chocolate cake, chocolate cookies?" He paused and added: "Chocolate buns?"

"What do you recommend?"

"I like chocolate buns myself."

"I'll take a dozen."

He left the room and soon returned with a box of glazed bread-rolls striped with a chocolate sauce.

"They look fine," I said.

When I paid, I noticed he was still smirking at me. He gave me my change and I just stood there, not knowing what to say.

"I guess you're all very busy these days," I said awkwardly.

"Not now. We do most of our sales in the morning and at lunch time."

"Oh," I said, eyes averted. I noticed his biceps bulging in his white t-shirt, the outline of an erect nipple above the top of his apron. I felt over-clothed, my collar pressing into my sweating neck.

"Would you like to see some buns out back?" he asked.

"What?"

"Chocolate buns. I can show you how they're made."

"Sure."

I followed him into the baking room. It was hot and humid and smelled of bread dough. I loosened my tie. All around were trays with chocolate-chip cookies on them. I saw a bowl full of hardening cake icing. "My assistants have left. We start baking really early in the morning." He showed me the stoves, working tables, washing area.

Then he just stood there facing me. He looked me up and down, sized up my double-breasted suit, my yellow silk tie.

Damn, I'd worn the tie-pin today. Do I have to look like a total nerd?

Suddenly he put one finger in a bowl of chocolate cake icing, smeared it across the center of my tie and laughed.

"What have you done?" I cried. He kept laughing. "You're going to have to pay to get this cleaned."

"Nice new stripe," he mocked. "Looks pretty stupid. Looks like you're just gonna have to take your tie off."

I didn't have to. He reached forward and in one quick movement, unknotted and pulled my tie from my neck. Then he flicked it in the air like a little whip, laughed and threw it in a big, silver bowl of cake batter. "Forget about your image, man," he said, pressing his hand against my rock-hard cock. "It's time for dessert."

He ripped off his apron, t-shirt, shoes and pants and stood before me, displaying his two unblemished butt-cheeks, lightly dimpled, a slight shadowing of hair down his beautiful crack. He reached over and took a handful of flour from a bowl and sprinkled it all over his bare ass.

"Dessert's ready," he said. "Seconds are allowed."

I couldn't believe it. I dove forward and pressed my face against his superbly muscled ass. I dug my teeth into his quivering butt-cheeks, shoved my face into his hot, moist crack, then swirled my tongue in his wonderful, throbbing crater. When I paused to catch my breath, he slathered chocolate icing all over his behind, then poured chocolate syrup down his crack and shoved a handful of chocolate chips up his butthole. I ate him out over and over, the taste of bakeshop goodies indistinguishable from his own succulent ass flavor. He added more syrup, more icing, more crumbled chocolate chips and I ate, gobbled and slathered. I must have gained ten pounds that day. Then, dizzy with excitement, on a sugar-high such as I've never felt in my life, I pulled out my hard dick, and using cake batter as lube, entered his tight, sticky hole and fucked him over and over.

When we were finished, my lips, cheeks, forehead, hair, shirt, Brooks Brothers jacket and pants were coated in his wonderful shit-chocolate mix.

I'm now a chocolate addict and could eat dessert morning, noon and night. I go to the bake-shop everyday after work and sometimes on Saturdays and Sundays, where his hungry hole and delectable sugared goodies are waiting to be devoured and savored.

Irish Moons

Harry Davis

Not every gay boy wants to go to Key West or West Hollywood, you know.

In this era of circuit parties and hedonistic resorts ubiquitously promoted as "clothing optional," there are still a few places where an outdoorsy, red-blooded all-American queer can camp in the great untamed wilds of America. Oh, I don't mean to camp in the contemporary vernacular sense, but in the old-fashioned literal sense, with tents, campfires and all that shit.

There's this place out by Palm Springs, in a canyon not that far from town but quite distant from the culture of martinis and lounging by the pool wrapped in a man-made mist. Nah, this is a real camp, run by a retired Air Force guy everyone calls Major Pop. Pops wasn't an officer though, just a plain old career tech sergeant. He has a rough, grizzled, enlisted man's look to him, too, with a graying buzz-cut, deeply set, wrinkly crevices from ear to ear and a purple scar that runs the length of his right cheek. Sadly, nowadays Pops spends most of his time behind the computer, managing Camp Hideout, where men, and men only, rent a tent and do a lot of hiking and other things in the pink sandy canyons that rise west of Palm Springs.

It's called communing with nature, and that includes with one another. When Pops's mallet-like hands aren't pumping the keyboard, they're handling jars of lube, poppers, and snake bite kits from under the counter. For ten bucks, you can get a day pass, which means you can commune, but can't stay overnight in one of Pops's canvas tents. It would also mean that you'd be missing out on the best reason for hiding out at the ole Camp Hideout.

Overnight guests are entitled to Major Pop's buckaroo breakfasts, an all you can eat type of affair laid out on trestle tables made from disused railroad ties. Major Pop believes in eating outdoors. All the cooking's done on a greasy, banged up grill, fueled by wood and coals in an oven built of boulders from the nearby arroyos. Around eight o'clock every morning, all the buckaroos set their butts on plank benches, share a cigarette and a tale or two, and gobble up pancakes, scrambled eggs, bacon, and fried potatoes. But enough about the food; let me tell you about the cook. The most salient thing is that the cook's bare-ass naked.

While he cooks.

The blue dime store bandana he wraps around his reddish brown hair doesn't count. Neither does his apron, since a cook's got to wear something, after all. So the cook's bare-ass naked.

This cook's a hot Irish looker who tends the grill wearing this full-length apron that loops over his head and ties around the waist, falling just short of his knees. But the apron does nothing to diminish the impact of this big built Irishman. His shoulders and forearms are tautly packed from years of manual labor. His skin is honed to a creamy matte finish, barren of hair but for a faint trail that travels from the neck and disappears in the small of his back.

He stands facing the grill, meaty thighs spread apart and big feet planted on a concrete slab-like a massive oak tree you'd want to crawl under. But right now, I'll settle for the nice view of those muscled shoulders, broad expanse of back, and that pair of fabulously rounded butt-cheeks, flawless without a blemish and so fine, white and firm. Farther south of those hard mounds of flesh are toned thighs and a pair of peat digger's legs that bulge everywhere they should, god almighty. Nobody misses breakfast with this cook. Call it the Morning Show, if you like. But, let's keep going down, farther down, all the way down. The cook has the manliest of feet. Beauties that are fat and wide, their calloused heels revealed by the heavy wooden clogs (his only other article of clothing besides the apron and bandana).

I always sought the most strategic location for getting a glimpse—as he crouched or bent over—of the soles of his feet and the sweat forming there. How I wanted to lick that hard, white flesh, starting with those big feet with their claw-like toes, curled and ready to clamp onto wool, moss or sand, and work my way up the hard outline of his calves, protruding from a million squats, across the columns of white meat growing from knee to crotch, until I'm there, on those heavenly Irish moons, full and round, slightly wet with butt-sweat, manly, and salty, never sweet.

"I know what you're thinking," said a voice in my ear. I turned, but there was nobody there. I resumed my little tour of muscular Ireland, but was jolted from my dream once again by a recurrent voice: "You can have that, if you want it."

Who said that? Who is this intruder who plays with my mind?

Nighttime brought a full moon, which is more significant in the desert than it might be elsewhere. In the desert, there are barriers of the white oleander, planted such that they gleam in the light of the moon. White they are, and they stand out amid the darkness, creating the atmosphere of the supernatural. One may wander in the foothills, among the massive blocks of sandstone, and see only these walls of white, unremarkable in daylight but all too obvious in the magic of the evening.

Such it was that evening as I wandered among the natural, landscaped decor of Camp Hideout. It was summer, it was warm, and there was the moonlight. "Go along that trail, deeper into the canyon," a voice whispered in the darkness. I looked over my shoulder; no one there. But I did venture on, my way lighted by the brightness of the full moon. There wasn't much farther to go before reaching the height of the foothill, where the bands of white oleander come to an abrupt end. And then, a clearing.

And there he was.

There was a tent at the head of the canyon, where he lay, prone and offered up to all who ventured there. I proceeded to his camp, flooded with moonlight yet sheltered by the local tamarisk, creating a maze of shadows, inviting, sexy. I saw a flash of white flesh in the darkness. "Go on," the voice said. I ventured farther. In the tent was my Irish god, his creamy white flanks spread to either side, as if posed by a great artist. I moved forward. I kneeled at the foot of the tent. I could touch very easily that firm white flesh that lay before me. It was hard, and glorious, and begging to be touched.

"Touch it," the voice ordered. I bent forward, hoping to catch the scent of this delightful white man's meaty skin, which glistened, however modestly, in the light of the desert moon. And then, I found myself at the edge of lovely man-lips, and they were protruding with dark and creviced ridges that bespoke of hours of manly fucking. Oh, how I wanted to put my lips on that gorgeous, full, plump man-flesh. Then, to my surprise, a shot of man-juice spurted from those pursing lips, quite unexpectedly, in a loud and sloppy shower.

I was taken aback. It was unexpected but not unwanted. Without hesitation I placed my tongue at the base of that fragrant, dripping asshole, anticipating the emission of more

manly and ebullient juices. And did it come, with unantici-
pated force, in rivulets of lush slag, sticky and lively as it
trailed from the quivering butthole to the base of his purple
balls. And did I lap it up, with strategic measure, with enthusiasm and religion, every clotting bit, each blob of living
jism. And then there came another spurt! How many loads
had been dumped into that white cum slot?

"Eat it," the voice said.

I buried my face in the crevice between those beautiful round Irish moons. I reveled in the scent of dick-juice
and sweat. I reveled in the flavor of tasty, meaty man-cunt
freshly fucked. I probed the deep duskiness of the puckered
hole that throbbed with each thrust of my tongue. Every man
in the camp had left a piece of himself in the deep, rich ass of
that piece of Ireland. Oh, god, let there be no doubt that I
had been entrusted with the duty of retrieving their leavings
and depositing it all deep within the vaults of my belly. With
my tongue I traversed the landscape of Ireland as I had come
to know it, licking up every trace of cum that had gone
astray, and then with equal vigor, proceeded to graze the salt
beds of sweat that shone in the moonlight.

The backside was explored, loved and made clean.
And finally, to the feet, hard and calloused from a lifetime
but still possessing the firmness and suppleness of well finished leather. I licked every bit of those fine, big feet, thinking of the white muscled ass they carried so well. From my
Irishman, there was not a stir.

"Go, now," the voice said. Reluctantly, I retreated,

walking backwards and never losing sight of the marble hill of white man-butt I had scaled. I retreated, in the moonlight, walking backwards in the desert until I lost sight of the dim figure, a white fire in the moonlit desert-scape. Behind me, the sun was rising.

With daybreak, we return to reality. The dreams, the passions and the fantasies of the night are lost with the coming of the dawn. And with morning comes Major Pop and pots of hot coffee. And now, I sit and contemplate the morning sun as it casts shadows on the mountains to the west, first purplish colors, then pink, before finally disappearing into a fierce, white light. And all around me, I can hear the voice, the voice of last night, repeating, repeating, "Good man, good man, so very good."

Baller's Booty

Donmika

I admit it. I am a butt-freak.

I turn into a two-month-old baby when I see a guy with a nice ass. No lie—blubbering, drooling, the works. I especially have a thing for light-skinned black ass, especially "baller's booty."

Brothers, y'all know what I'm talking 'bout, right?

Baller's Booty is when a brother has a nice muscular torso, slender waist—usually from working out or playing ball—strong legs, muscular thighs ... and the booty—damn! That ass sticking out nice and firm ... kind of makes the back look like it's curving.

My baby, Ernesto, has the epitome of baller's booty.

I met him at our first track practice and watched his pretty ass from the moment he stepped on the field. I had never seen an ass so firm and round. That's probably why I ran like crap that day. My mind was *not* on track. I was much too busy tying to remember the theme songs to cartoons, which was the only way I could keep from springing wood. If I'd've gotten an erection, it would have been all over for Ernesto. I would have peeled those tight spandex shorts off his muscular thighs and ass and dicked that Puerto Rican pussy right then and there on the track—maybe hit it so hard I would've put an end to his athletic career.

The first time he opened those pretty pink lips to speak during that first practice, I figured that ass could be had. Despite his cornrows and thuggish looks, his voice was far from manly; but it wasn't exactly feminine either. It sounded more like a twelve-year-old prior to puberty, occasionally accented with a lisp. Under normal circumstances, I would have found this highly annoying. But seeing as how he had graced me with the site of that ass, his voice didn't bothered me much.

As track season went on, Ernesto and I discovered that we had a lot more in common than we ever could've imagine. We became best friends and told each other shit that we never breathed to another soul. I found out that Ernesto was also a freak for athletic ass, but his fetish was slightly different from my own. He lived for the smell of a sweaty ass and loved to sniff and lick my ass when I came home from playing ball or running track. Turned out, Ernesto was a bigger butt-freak than me in some ways.

But not when it came to actually fucking booty. He

froze up, which suited me just fine. You see, Ernesto and I were truly made for each other. Both of us were sexually abused in our early teens, which might explain some of our hang-ups with sex. In my opinion, Ernesto was the luckier. Three girls from his neighborhood held him down and took turns with him. They claimed he was too cute to be gay and that they could make him like pussy. *Wrong!*

As for me, an older male cousin raped me from the time I was sixteen to when I left for college. When he died this past spring, I told my grandmother about him and she cried, deciding that my bisexuality was the result of what he did to me. She was wrong though. I was always bi. All he did was make me damn sure I never wanted to get fucked again.

It's a shame, too, because I have a great ass. When I was younger, I would stand in the mirror and check out my booty for hours. I'd spread my cheeks and peek between my legs to look at my hole while I jerked off. I would definitely fuck my own butt if I could. I even tried it once. My ass is an irresistible little brown onion. I've had to stop more than one female from getting carried away and sticking a finger in it. I hate anything touching my ass, or at least, I used to.

Okay, now for the part you've been waiting for (maybe what you skipped the rest of my story for), one of our many sexual encounters. . . .

Ernesto startled as I opened the front door and entered the living room. His face was red. He was on his back, butt-naked on the couch. A porno was on the tube and he was struggling to remove a giant black dildo from his rectum.

"Started without me?" I said laughingly, then walked over to the sofa and grabbed his arm, preventing him from removing the dildo. "Go on, baby, show off for your nigga. Let me see how much of that shit you can handle."

Without a word, his hand forced more of the thirteen-by-five penile replica into his ass. He grimaced and instantly, my dick poked out from under the leg of my cutoff sweats. Encouraged, Ernesto's ass swallowed the dildo whole. Then he rolled onto his stomach, nestled his face into my crotch and began nibbling my dick shaft through the cotton. Next, he teased my exposed cockhead with his tongue and I reached behind him to spread his greasy cheeks.

"Oh-fuck!" he said, removing the dildo. His ass let out a wet, greasy sound as he turned around on all fours to give me a view of his gaping hole. I ran my index finger from the curve of his back to the length of his moist slit and inserted a knuckle into his gaper.

Damn! That got me so hot, I couldn't contain my urge to dick him down any longer. I yanked off my shorts.

"Fuck me," he purred, throwing himself on his back. His booty was tooted up toward me, the gaping, pink hole begging to be filled. Good thing he was already lubed up from the dildo: I didn't want to waste any more time outside his love-tunnel. I swabbed my dick up and down the length off his slit until my cock was shining from the lube and natural moisture of his ass. Finally, I lined the head up against his swollen rim.

"You want it all?" I teased, leaving the tip at his entrance.

"Hell, yeah."

"Then hold them yellow cheeks apart."

I loved to watch his rim fold inward as I pushed the tip of my dick in. That was my favorite part of sex. He did as he was told. I smiled and pushed my dick a little farther in.

"Beg for it," I told him.

"Come on, baby." He spread his cheeks wider. "Please, baby. Gimme that big dick, *papi*."

That was enough bull-shitting for both of us. I always caved into his New York Spanish accent. I had to give it to him like he wanted it: rough and violent.

"Bring that pussy here, boy!" I grabbed his shoulders and pulled him into my dick.

"Ahhh, shit!" he groaned. I pulled out and slammed back in so hard, his cheeks made a smacking noise against my balls.

"You want this dick, boy?" I leaned back to watch the base of my jet-black cock against his pubic hairs.

"Ahhh, shit!" he squirmed.

I gave his ass a pop with my hand and his hole tightened around my dick. I did it again. And again . . . and again . . . until his ass-cheek was red with my handprints. He began crying like a little bitch, which made me even hotter.

"I thought you wanted this big dick!" I said, grabbing him by his cornrows. "Toss me that pussy, nigga!"

"Ahhh, fuck, *papi*, you killin' me."

I fucked him so hard, my nuts stung from the impact of my body crashing into his ass. Then, after a good long while, I decided to let him take control.

"Make me cum," I ordered him.

He rocked back and forth, rotating his pelvis and pushing his ass into my dick. I leaned back and held the base of my cock in my hand as he pushed more and more of his red-hot rim onto me. He slang his ass balls-deep onto my dick and tightened and loosened his ass muscles, milking me like a baby with a bottle.

"You going to give me that hot cum?" he begged, working harder to bring me to climax. "Give me them black babies, boy! I want you to spray my guts!"

"I will, boy!" I slapped his ass again. "Just keep going. I'm almost there."

He obeyed. I loosened my grip on his cheeks, causing them to jiggle back into place.

"Here it goes, boy!" I forced myself deeper into his hole. "I'm cummin' boy! Oh, shit . . . .ahhh, fuck!"

"Oh, shit, *papi!*" he screamed. "Give me them babies! Nut all in my stomach and shit!"

I shot jets of my shit all up inside him. I was still shooting several seconds later when I snatched out. After I was all the way out, Ernesto got on his knees, turned around and spread his cheeks to give me a view of my cum spilling out of his swollen rim. I forced him back down and rammed what was left of my erection back into his mushy hole. I cursed everything under God's creation, and after I was sure

I could release no more, pulled out and watched him squirm as my cum bubbled past his rim and down his thighs.

"Good boy!" I leaned down and kissed the back of his neck.

He reached behind me and positioned my dick between his ass-cheeks like a hot dog in a bun while I massaged my cum into the beautiful, golden skin of his butt.

"Shoot that shit, boy!" I said as he jerked himself with my dick between his buns. "Be a good boy. Shoot that shit, nigga."

"I need your help."

"Big baby," I said teasingly, then leaned forward, kissed his shoulder blades and wrapped my hand around his cock.

"No," he said. "Not this. You know what I need."

"*Aiiright,*" I sighed. He wanted to give me a rim-job, which I hated with a passion. But he had just broken me off with a proper nut, so how could I deny his request? I leaned across the wooden coffee table and he ran his fingers against my furry slit.

"Damn, you all sweaty and sticky," he announced with jubilation. I closed my eyes. He buried his face deep between my dark brown cheeks and his tongue worked its way into my hole. The sound of him jerking off became louder and faster.

"You nuttin'?" I asked, looking over my shoulders. He grabbed my waist and tugged at the patch of hair around my rim with his teeth. His way of putting me on notice to not interrupt him. "Shit," I groaned. I was just about to tell him to get his nut another way when he began breathing heavily.

"Oh, fuck!" he said as a series of hot jets hit my thighs and calves. When the splashes stopped, he collapsed against my back, panting like a dog and grinding his cum into my ass and thighs with his torso.

"You love that freaky shit, huh?" I laughed in disgust. He leaned forward to kiss me as his leaking dick shriveled back into its foreskin against my ass.

"I love you, Ashlie," he whispered, resting his head on my back.

"I love you, too." I closed my eyes and savored the image of that firm, red ass being pulled apart, the hole gaping with moist, pink flesh, begging to be filled.

Ernesto sprawled out on the floor on his stomach. His cum-covered ass was tilted toward the heavens, like a photo from our large collection of erotic magazines. I couldn't resist lying beside him and massaging his ass until it soothed us both to sleep.

Thank God, for brothers with baller's booties.

Tongue and Arse

Ian Parques

I was fifteen when I felt someone's tongue lick my arsehole for the first time. The sensation was unbelievable. It beat the first time I'd touched another cock, the first time I'd tasted dick, the first time I swallowed cum or the first time I was fucked. I didn't realise then that doing the licking was an even better high.

Gary was three years older than me, but because of ill health, he was a couple of years behind in his education and was therefore in my class at school. Due to our mutual lack of interest in sport, we became friends, as instead of taking part in football or cricket, we were made to go cross country running. As we were based in the middle of London "cross country" was a little misleading. We would pound the streets in the area near the sports field, dressed in white cotton shorts and T-shirts. My eyes would frequently wander to the bulge in Gary's shorts and it wasn't long before he noticed my interest.

One day, while walking down a narrow alleyway (we only "ran" until we were out of sight of our teachers), he asked if I had ever felt another boy's dick. I swallowed hard, said that I had, and very casually, he asked if I wanted to feel his. Did I?! We stopped and he lowered his shorts. It was obvious that ill health had not stunted his growth in any way. He wasn't hard, but his prick was about seven inches long and beautifully shaped with a shiny purple head. His hairy balls hung low and were the largest I'd ever seen. (But then to be honest, despite what I told Gary, I hadn't really *seen* that many.)

I was already hard, and soon my fingers were gripping his dick and his fingers were gripping mine. We wanked each other off and that was the start of a beautiful friendship.

Whereas once I dreaded sports afternoons, now I couldn't wait. As the weeks progressed, we became more adventurous. We stopped putting on underwear beneath our running shorts, which to us was highly erotic. Then we began to arrange our shorts so that the tips of our cocks peeked out. The amount of dick showing increased each week. How we got away with it, I still don't know. Our shorts were often soaked with pre-cum just from looking at each other's dicks. We experimented with sucking each other off, fingering, and on a couple of occasions back in the changing room, fucking.

My first rimming experience occurred one afternoon

in the changing room. As usual, we were back before the other boys. We had both cum and were still naked. I stood up and reached for my bag off the top of the locker when I felt Gary's hands on my backside. Then he was kissing my arse checks, which I enjoyed, but I was completely taken by surprise when he began to kiss my arse crack, pulling it apart with his hands. When I felt his tongue lick my crack and push into my hole, I thought I would explode. His tongue probed farther and with my initial resistance melting, my muscles relaxed. I could feel his hot breath and his wet tongue sliding in deeper. I leaned forward, pushing my backside out, and Gary's tongue went in even farther. I could not believe the feeling. It was better than anything I had ever experienced before.

For some reason, we never did it again, but I kept fantasizing about the experience. It was the only thing I thought about when I was wanking on my own—but not thoughts about a tongue up my arse, but *my* tongue up a backside. I was desperate to try sticking my tongue in some man's arsehole. It became a constant sexual thought. But I didn't do anything about it for a number of years. Gary left school and we soon lost touch. I had other sexual encounters—all fun— but I never felt at ease enough to position my mouth near another boy's or man's arse crack. None of my sex partners rimmed me, so the opportunity to return the favour didn't arise. It was, however, becoming a preoccupation of mine. Looking at underwear advertisements in magazines, I would imagine what the arse underneath—and more importantly, the actual hole—looked like. I finally found some porn magazines with photos of guys rimming. My favourite ones were the hairy arse shots taken just after a tongue had been withdrawn and saliva could be seen matting the arse hair together. Even though it was a major fantasy, I still wasn't sure whether I would like the reality of it or not.

An opportunity finally arose when I was 18. I met a French guy around my age in a pub. We got to talking and it soon became obvious that we both wanted to have sex without any strings. Perhaps that was what made me feel more relaxed, knowing that this was sex only and that was all we both wanted. We could do what we wanted without shocking the other person, and if it was something we didn't want to do, no offence would be taken.

We had nowhere to go, so I took the risk of taking him back to where I worked, which was open around the clock. I walked a little behind him so that I could look at his arse, which was well shaped. He was wearing thin summer trousers and no underwear and the material clung to his buttocks, showing off the crack. I had a key to a stock room and when the coast was clear, we slipped in. With some light shining through a small window, we got down to business. He wasn't an Adonis (mind you neither am I), but he had a reasonably good body, small dick, and tight balls. As we undressed, I positioned myself so that when he bent over to remove his trousers I could get a clear view of his butt. Even in the half-light, I could see that he had a hairy crack and I was determined to get a closer look.

I thought I ought to take it slowly, so I moved down to lick his balls and suck his dick. The aroma of piss that hit me was almost overpowering. Instead of being a turnoff, I became even more excited. It was such a sexual smell and above all, it indicated that he could be into what I then thought of as dirty sex. I took his prick in my mouth and was able to take it all so that my nose was pressed into his piss-soaked pubic hair. The aroma was intoxicating. I was now even more determined to explore that arse with my tongue. There were momentary fears that, given his lack of hygiene, his backside might be rank, but I felt it was a risk worth taking.

There could always be a tactical withdrawal.

He was totally passive, although obviously enjoying himself, which was just what I wanted. It didn't appear that he would object to anything being done to him, providing he did not have to respond in kind. In other circumstances, this probably would have annoyed me, but not on this occasion. I let his cock slip out of my mouth and licked my way down to his balls. I almost came with excitement at the pleasure of sucking on his piss-soaked balls. It was as if he had washed them in urine. The smell and taste was out of this world, but the best was yet to come.

After awhile, I moved my tongue down below his balls, licking between his legs. He arched his back (the most movement he had made so far), and I could see my prize. I knelt between his legs and inched my tongue nearer to his hole. I thought I was going to die from excitement. The tip of my tongue touched his hairy crack. My first lick of an arse! It was sweaty but clean and tasted sweet. I breathed in and for the first time could smell that wonderful smell of a man's arse. A smell that never fails to turn me on. No matter how clean, there is a special smell and taste that remains with you, reminding you that you have tasted the most intimate part of a man.

I'd done it. Once my tongue had reached it's target, there was no stopping me. I licked the hairs and could feel the soft skin underneath. I pushed my tongue against the hole and it gave way like magic. I went in as far as I could go, almost suffocating myself in the progress. The French guy was obviously enjoying himself and opened his hole wider by pulling on his cheeks. We repositioned ourselves so that he was squatting over me and for the first time, I got a proper view of his arse and the prized shithole. I couldn't believe that it could be so beautiful. It was as hairy as I had first thought, but the hair was concentrated around the actual opening. I could have looked at that butt for hours. I still like to look at an arsehole before I go into it. They all look different, some more attractive than others, but all opening up to a probing tongue.

I licked around the hole, getting his arse hair soaking wet. I pulled his cheeks apart with my hands and the hole opened even wider. I couldn't stop myself and lunged straight in with my tongue, getting in even farther than before. I played with that crack with my tongue for nearly an hour and every minute was bliss. We changed positions several times, some of them giving me more access than others (those were the ones I preferred). My friend couldn't get enough; I had a feeling that he had done this before. Eventually, neither one of us could hold back any longer and I could feel his arse tighten around my tongue as he came with much noise and mess. It wasn't long before I joined him.

From that moment my sex life—no my *life*—was never the same again. And I'm not just referring to the aching jaw I had for a number of days afterwards.

I wasn't shy any more about making rimming a major part of my sex life. I had never been keen on fucking. What a waste of such an inviting hole—shoving a dick in it—when you can explore it with a tongue and feel that part of a man that even *he* doesn't get to see properly. Rimming gives such pleasure to both the active and passive partner, and while I don't dislike being rimmed, I am happiest with my nose pressed against an arse and my tongue up it.

As the years have progressed, my fascination with arses has not diminished. I love looking at a male backside and imagining what that wonderful opening tastes and smells like. Nowadays, I have become used to arses that are not always as clean as I would like and can cope quite admirably. It is, after all, still a hairy, puckered arsehole. How can that be a turnoff? I don't think I have ever turned down the opportunity to probe a crack with my very willing tongue. I am not into scat, which many people associate with rimming, but I have to be honest and say that the thought that my tongue is cleaning out a shithole is a major mind fuck and part of the joy. What can be more intimate than using your tongue to clean the inside a man's crack?

Having someone sit on your face, opening their arse crack as wide as it will go, darting your tongue in and out, licking the anal hairs, dribbling, smelling that man smell, knowing that your tongue has entered an area so private that usually only shit comes out of it, is one of the most erotic, sexual experiences imaginable.

Thanks, Gary, for showing me the way!

Rimming Kevin

Bryce Marr

Quite a number of years ago, while still in my teens, I started getting into bodybuilding in a big way. With time, I discovered my fascination for physical male strength. In my early twenties, I drifted occasionally into a few gay clubs and really got off on getting my muscles worshipped. Sitting on some guy's face and having my asshole rimmed and tongued out real good made all that working-out seem worthwhile. I never thought I would ever get off on licking some other guy's butthole until, after just turning thirty-one, I had an encounter with what I think must be the most hunky young muscle-stud I've ever laid eyes on.

On my way to work while living in small town Australia, I passed by a small plot of land where some sort of landscape garden was being built. There just seemed to be this one guy working on it and was he something. I reckon he must have been in his mid-twenties, a little short of two meters tall, short blond hair, and made of a hell of a lot of solid muscle. Because of the hot weather, he only wore a pair of tight-fitting, torn-off jeans and was showing off his hard bronzed body: huge biceps, massive shoulders and chest and bulging muscular thighs (I had never seen quadriceps like those before). It was amazing just to watch him work, this awesome specimen of masculinity, to see him shoveling cement, flexing his huge hard muscles and bending over occasionally, showing off his tight buttocks through the fabric of his shorts and letting the sunlight reflect off the massive frame of his back.

I used to take as many breaks from work as I could in order to admire him, getting one hard-on after another and practically cumming at the mere thought of his gorgeous tight butt.

One afternoon, while he was taking a break—sitting on the fence that he was in the process of building, eating a sandwich and showing off his bulging biceps—I plucked up my courage and went up to him, trying to seem as calm, casual and as normal as possible.

"Ya got a big job there, mate?" I asked.

"Aw yeah," he answered in a deep rustic baritone voice, "about another week and I reckon I'll have it finished."

"Aw yeah? You're a fucking big cunt, mate; you'll have it finished sooner, I reckon. You're bloody strong enough." I gave him a matey sort of a punch on the shoulder. "Fuck, ya gotta workout a hell of a lot to get looking like you do."

"Aw yeah, I've been lifting for about eleven, twelve years. Yeah, since I was about fifteen. It's for the footy season, you know, man."

We began to talk in a familiar way about recent rugby league matches and players. I knew that I wasn't going to be able to control my excitement for too much longer. He was a real rugged, down-to-earth, tough sort of guy and I was a bit scared about how he might react to any sort of sexual advances. His fierce looking eyes and stubbly, lantern-jawed face intimidated me slightly, but I was feeling too reckless to back off. Finally, when I felt certain that this brawny young hunk in front of me was too humored to get aggressive, I came out with my proposition:

"Alright then, ya big rugby dude, how would ya like to sit on my face before ya get back to work, eh?"

He looked at me a little puzzled and for a split second, I really did think that he might beat me up. Then he grinned a manly grin and laughed.

"Aw yeah, if ya can lick good ass, c'mon round the back."

Amazed at my luck, I followed him across the section, gazing transfixed at his muscular back, butt and calves as he swaggered over to his small wooden tool shed. Once we were inside, he locked the door. There were no windows: a large piece of transparent Perspex in the ceiling let in the light. He looked even more awesome and more massive in such a small closed room. I inhaled the sweaty, intoxicatingly musky scent of brute manliness which exuded from every pore of his hard, chiseled body. He leaned back against a wall.

He was magnificent.

"If ya wanna eat my ass, dude, ya gotta suck on this first!" he ordered in a gruff voice, unzipping his shorts and flopping out his meaty thick cock. I took off my shirt and kneeled before him. He bent his powerful knees slightly so that I could get better access to his dick. I went down on him, trying my best to take as much of his thick man-meat into my mouth and down my throat as I could. His cock responded immediately to my attentions, growing larger and larger.

"Yeah, dude, yeah," moaned my big blond muscle-god.

I clasped my hands on his massive bronzed thighs, feeling his incredible strength through my fingertips. He grasped my head on either side with his strong hands and pushed me down farther on his enormous ten-incher while thrusting it simultaneously down my throat. I choked and spluttered, doing my best to take the big round head of his thick cock as far down my throat as I could. While I gagged on his cock, my hands wandered over his hard rugged body, touching and feeling his washboard abs, smooth massive chest, nipples, and of course, his amazingly tight firm buns. Having deep-throated him as best I could, I then licked up and down the shaft of his meaty long cock for a while, teasing his balls with my tongue and showing my eagerness to get farther underneath him.

"Ya wanna eat my ass now, man, huh?" he said in his

deep husky voice. I looked up at him in anticipation, surveying his mighty chest and powerfully broad shoulders. He had
a big horny grin on his face that made me feel all the more
turned on. Helping him pull his shorts off over his working
boots, I was on fire watching every movement of his heavily
muscled body as he slowly turned around and bent over.
What a fucking awesome sight that was: those massive
bronzed shoulders leaning forward, those feet shoulder-
width apart, those powerful muscular legs slightly bent at the
knee, and that delicious looking ass-crack within tongue's
reach. Still kneeling, I shuffled forward, parted this hunky
young landscaper's firm smooth muscled ass-cheeks gently
with my hands and stared into his small pink shaven asshole.
It seemed so tiny in comparison to the rest of this studly
giant. Without hesitating, I plunged my face into his sweaty
ass-crack and started to lick slowly up and down.

"Fuck! Yeah!" he moaned. He clasped the back of my
head with his brawny right hand, forcefully pushing and
rubbing my face and tongue farther into his ass. I pulled his
ass-cheeks as far apart as they would go, pushed the tip of my
tongue into his clean puckered little butthole as far as I could
and really sucked with all my strength. The sweaty masculine
taste and aroma of this young hunk's ass was like taking a
drug that instantly threw me into a total sexual frenzy.
Encouraged by his deep manly groans, I kept on licking,
sucking and chewing hungrily at this muscleman's asshole,
occasionally stroking my own cock, which was aching to
explode. Little by little, his tight little butthole began to

loosen up a bit, enabling me to ram my tongue in deeper and deeper.

"Aaw yeah!" he grunted. "I'm gonna sit on ya face now, man." He shunted me backwards with his ass and stood upright. I lay down on the floor between his beefy legs, admiring his muscular butt, back and shoulders as he slowly crouched down into a squatting position directly above my face. Fuck, what a turn-on it was to see that awesome pair of glutes descend toward me, opening up to reveal the moist glistening rosebud of that pre-licked asshole that I was going to deep-tongue and eat out. Positioning his hot, breathing butthole directly over my mouth, my big blond muscle-stud pressed his ass into my face, locking me between his asshole and the floor. He sure knew how to get the most out of an ass-eater's services! Wild with the smell and the taste of his butt, I started pigging out on his sphincter, which (rewarding my efforts) began to give way, opening up more and more and allowing my insatiable tongue to probe deeper into this young muscleman's rectum. My jaw was aching, but I was too excited to care: I just wanted to bury my tongue as far into this perfect ass as it could possibly go.

"Fuck, yeah, eat me out, man . . . yeah!"

I would've loved to have been able to see the lusty expression on his face. Squatting on my mouth, this young titan seemed to be able to contract his ass muscles in such a way that his butthole seemed to suck my tongue up farther inside him. My tongue responded eagerly to these contractions, wriggling and twisting its way deeper and deeper into this blond muscle-god's tight ass canal. With my fingertips, I could touch and feel his massive powerful thighs heaving away above me as he continued to grind his ass unrelentingly into my face. Moaning with pleasure, he seemed to be jerking off his thick ten-incher with one hand and squeezing his nipples with the other.

"Yeah, man, eat that ass, man, eat that ass!"

I was almost suffocating underneath him. I started cumming in my pants, feelings as if all his weight and Herculean strength were centered around my tongue, as if I were swallowing and inhaling all of this muscular giant through my wide-open mouth. With my entire tongue buried deep inside his hot sweaty asshole, he too seemed to be reaching his climax. With a mighty roar, he began to cum. Under the force of his orgasm, his tight muscular asshole seemed to clasp my tongue and I could feel his heavy warm wads of cum fall onto my chest. I kept my tongue buried inside his butthole while he began to cool down a bit. Rubbing his ass in my face and letting me lick over his asshole one last time, he stood up slowly and seemed a little dizzy and his legs a bit stiff after so much excitement and exertion in a squatting position.

"Gee thanks, mate," he said, looking at me with embarrassment.

"Anytime," I answered, wiping the cum of my chest and rubbing my tired jaw.

The name of this brute mass of brawn was Kevin. And while he was working on that section of land, he let me service him quite often. After this encounter, I launched a sexual career as a butt-eating muscle worshipper who appreciates muscle butts that like some real good ass-licking attention.

No reciprocation necessary.

Just enjoy.

Booty on the Men I Love

The BGM Poet

It's lickable, suckable and smellable. That's why I love butt so much.

There are two types of booty I enjoy most.

Number one is Latino butt. My first experience with *culo Latino* was at a bathhouse in LA. This *papi chulo* came to my room with a booty that was all that: nice, firm, round, yellow. It was also hairy and ripe for pounding. I slide my fingers inside his manhole and he moaned with intense pleasure. I lubricated his hole with my pre-cum and played with that *culo peludo,* licking and eating to my hearts content. Eventually, I pounded his manhole with my dick. Later, he came back for seconds.

I was glad he did. His hairy hole was delicious.

The second kind of butt I find erotic is *azz* from my own peeps: black man's booty. I enjoy seeing my bruthas' booties during the summer time, walking and playing b-ball. Black azz is best when it's firm, round, soft, tight, muscular, dark, chocolate, red, light-brown, plump. I love sucking a black man's hole and making him scream for more.

Right then and there, I'm making him my man.

I enjoy smelling my man's hole and tasting his azz juices. Playing with it deeply. Exploring it. I enjoy seeing him naked in the shower with soap running down the crack of his ass.

I also enjoy it when a brutha puts his lips on *my* booty, which makes me *holla holla*. I'm usually a bottom and enjoy having my fat booty pounded long and deep for hours by a deserving top man. I love it when a guy cums in my manhole. Or should I say my boy-pussy?

Well, I'm wet now and no lube was needed. I must close this out and go have a huge, good ole bootilicious time. Oh, what joy it is to talk about a man's butt.

What *booty* it is to be a part of the gay world and its culture.

Going Somewhere

Gregory Woods

I first saw him on a tube train. He was standing at the door,
Trying to look sophisticated, scornful, sexy. Ears plugged
With music. I didn't see him till I saw him smile. His mouth
Oozed like peach flesh. I followed the smile down the carriage to where
A man in his forties or fifties was sitting, craning his

Neck, transfixed. They played the game of looking and looking away.
The smile came and went like ripeness with the seasons. Their timing
Broke: each looked when the other was looking away. At East Finchley
I stood up to get out. The boy got out before me. I followed
Him to the stairs. Just once he looked back to see if the man had

Left the train. I looked too. No. Didn't dare. When the crowd thickened
To go down the stairs I went right up behind him. We started
Down the steps and my left thigh hit his butt. To keep him from falling
Forward I grabbed his arm. People passed round us on both sides.
When I said sorry he stopped looking scared and went on down the steps.

Outside the station he turned right on the high road and walked to
A bus stop under the railway bridge. He joined the long queue.
I stood next to him. I was thinking about his arse, wondering
If it would repay the effort. His jeans were cheap and loose, but
I could guess the shape. Pronounced. It was half six and people were

Going home, breathing winter breath. Our queue became a crowd
Before the bus arrived. I guessed an old man with liver spots
Would get in my way when the time came, and sure enough he did.
The boy jumped the queue, flashing his pass at the driver. He went
Upstairs, but I didn't get to follow his arse on the stairs

Because I had to help the old man onto the bus. He dropped
His stick. Someone was pushing me from behind. Although the seat
In front of the boy was empty I sat next to him. He was
Looking out at the end of the queue fighting to get on board.
I spread my legs so my thigh would touch his. I unzipped my new

Leather jacket. It was making me feel more confident than
Usual. I reached into my shirt pocket for my cigarettes,
Took one myself and offered him one. He looked at me quick and
Took it. Oily fingers with nails bitten to the quick. "Thanks, mate."
I lit it for him. We both knew our legs were still touching, both

Knew why. "Where you getting out?" I asked. "Where you like." We got out
At the next stop and walked back to the station, bumping shoulders.
I had cut an appointment. It was for a Chinese meal with
Someone I liked. I would make it up to her another time.
"Were you going somewhere important?" "Only home," he muttered.

He was still living with his parents. Cypriots. I took him
Back to my place and opened some wine. By the time we knew each
Other's name we were down to our shorts, our cockheads touching through
Slimy cotton. We took it in turns to spit in each other's
Mouth. His armpits and groin were giving off a gamey smell.

He talked about Cyprus and the Greeks and the Turks and sang me
A meaningful song. I spat in him when he was singing the
Long last note. It dribbled down his chin. When I asked if I could
Eat his arse you never saw anyone move so quick. He was
Out of his shorts in a flash and lying facedown on the bed.

He said he liked it best from men with beards. I arranged him so
His legs were apart and his cock was pointing down the bed at mine.
I looked till he grew impatient. "Come on, man." I slapped him. He
Clenched his butt and a pearl of goo squeezed out of his dick. So I
Hit him again. The cheeks were starting to blush. He hid his face

In the pillow. I hid mine in him. Straight away he was moaning.
At times like this I wonder what people would think of me. A man
In his thirties with his tongue up a nineteen-year-old's arsehole.
Just a moment of scandal, then I forget who I am. The taste
Takes over. How can you think of anything but living meat?

Romancing the Asshole

James Francis

The intense heat of the day was over. A cool breeze heralded the arrival of evening as surely as the lengthening shadows. I walked up the hill toward the park, wondering if I would remember this night or if it would just be another disappointment.

Forest Park, its old growth trees towering over a multitude of secluded paths, was my destination. The cool breeze ruffled the hair on my chest, teasing my nipples through my silky tank top, which I knew showed off my hairy pecs to perfection.

I turned onto Lawrence Lane, built during the 1920s as yet another promenade for the newly wealthy neighborhood of Kew Gardens. Now, it was slightly frayed along the edges, rumored to be the cruisiest section of the park.

Intermittent street lamps guided me onto a wide slate path surrounded by dense, overgrown shrubbery and massive trees. I could see vague shadows and outlines of human bodies. At first glance, they seemed innocent enough. However, closer inspection of the writhing images revealed that the woods were full.

Full of cocksucking, butt-fucking and all manner of man-on-man action. The kind of place I had been looking for all my life.

I was an adolescent and this would be my first visit to this infamous cockfest. For many months now, I had struggled to hide my erections when others spoke of what went on at Larry's Lane, feigning disinterest while my mind sifted through the stories for usable information. Did gay guys really congregate in the park? What time of day? Was it only at night? How did they dress? How did this whole thing get started anyway?

The more I considered these questions, the more the nagging fear that I *might* be gay melted into a white-hot determination to have man-sex. I needed to hold another man in my arms, to make out and make love with someone who really turned me on. And finally lose my despised cherry. Sure, I had tried before. Trying to find a man (any man really) to share myself with had been my top priority for months. I listened raptly every time any mention was made of gays or homos, trying to fill in the blanks. I had even scored an old dog-eared copy of *Mandate* magazine from the dumpster behind the drugstore. I jerked my cock sore, star-

ing at the rugged, masculine men who had posed naked for
the pleasure of other men.

Still I wanted more. The physical release wasn't
enough to satisfy my need to love another man. In despera-
tion, I began to sneak into the Adult Love Boutique on
Queens Boulevard. In this tacky, smelly, mostly straight
emporium, I finally had sex with a man, or at least found
some cock to suck. The dicks belonged to mostly straight
dudes who were horny enough to let anyone suck them off
after a couple of hours of watching porno videos in the quarter booths.

I learned what a glory hole was and how to use it,
although I preferred the body contact that a face-to-face session provided. I was tall for my age, and good looking, so if I
could slip past the sales clerk, I usually scored a blowjob or
two before they threw me out. I would suck a stranger's cock,
jerking myself off at the same time. Or let him blow me if he
liked dick, too. Some of the guys were friendly. They introduced me to poppers and Rush (which blew my mind, the
orgasms stretching out to what seemed like minutes). Some
gave me extra quarters so that I could stay in the buddy
booths longer without getting caught.

But it was ass that filled my adolescent soul with long-
ing. As I gave blowjobs, I would try to hold onto the guy's
ass-cheeks so that I could sniff my fingers and jerk off again
later. I also spent more than my share of time servicing balls.
They were so close to the little pink hole of my dreams. But
everybody always pushed my hand away, afraid that I was

trying to start some anal action. "Sorry, I'm not into that," they said over and over. But on a boring school day, when I overheard Tom Dooley and Joey Pugliesi laughing about Larry's Lane being "Ass Fuck Alley for the queers," I knew I had discovered "the place" at last.

So now, dressed for seduction, trying to look older and more sure of myself than I felt, I walked into the increasing darkness. Bracketing the path, trees cast surreal shadows, sheltering the groupings of men, hiding them from our prying eyes.

"Fuck yeah, man . . . suck my dick . . . oh, yeah . . . .I'm gonna cum."

I could hear the slurping and groaning of man-on-man action. My dick swelled with excitement. Even the smells were intoxicating. The leafy aroma of the forest intertwined with different colognes, man-sweat and poppers, filling my senses with images of the spermfest I hoped awaited me.

The path got narrower as it went on. Guys passed me in both directions. Some deliberately passed too close, surreptitiously brushing my nipples, cupping my ass or fondling my bulge for brief, sexy moments. Men had never touched me like this in front of others before. I decided I liked it. It excited me that everyone here knew that I fucked around with guys. It was my first flash of gay pride.

My eyes tried to focus in the increasing darkness. I could only see flashes of the action: a kneeling man here, another lolling against a tree trunk playing with his cock, men soul-kissing in groups. The sight of four handsome dudes swapping spit in a sexy four-way kiss, right out in the open, not caring who saw them, set my hormones into over-drive.

Guy after guy passed. From hairless blonds in Day-Glo disco attire to burly daddies wearing business suits—their shirts open to the navel to reveal hairy chests—the parade of men went on and on. Some of them refused my gaze, look-ing away before our eyes met. In others, I sensed interest as our eyes locked briefly, then moved on to the next contes-tant.

This mating dance intrigued me. It almost seemed choreographed. We all walked slowly, staring at one another briefly, sweaty muscles, hairy chests, bulging baskets all vying for attention. I walked on with determination.

The path narrowed yet again, the slate of the walkway giving way to grass. Moonlight replaced the dim lamplight as the only illumination. This darker area attracted fewer but more adventurous types. The figures wrestling among the trees were now naked rather than half dressed and the moan-ing was less muffled. I sensed that the primary activity here had shifted beyond sucking dick. Fucking was definitely in the air.

A tree root, invisible in the darkness, snagged my foot.

A strong arm broke my fall and held me up by my arms.

"Easy does it." He was so close, I felt his warm breath on my face.

"Thanks, man." I tried to pull away as I regained my balance, but his grip remained firm. His face was handsome. He smiled slightly, revealing nice, even teeth. He tossed back his mane of black hair and touched my chest. But it was his shirtless torso, hairy and muscular, that made my cock jump for joy.

"Don't go . . . yet." He put an arm around my shoulders. His cologne matched his masculine physique.

"I was looking for . . . a friend," I mumbled, my voice hoarse with lust.

His good-natured laugh filled the air and he turned me so that I was facing him.

"Can't we be . . . friends, too?"

I turned my head upward and his lips brushed mine. Our tongues met and I melted into his strong masculine embrace. We kissed passionately.

Instinctively, my hand reached for his cock. It was then that I realized that this hunky man in my arms was totally naked. His hand slipped inside the waistband of my jeans; I found his manhole—hot, moist and seemingly waiting for my touch. Electricity coursed through my cock as his hand touched my ass-crack. When he slipped his finger inside me, my knees buckled.

I kissed my way down his neck to his hairy chest as I massaged his cock shaft with his pre-cum. He groaned as my teeth found his nipple. "Fuck yeah," he said as my head bowed lower. His belly was as hairy as his chest and he loved the way I licked my way past his belly button. He was leaking even more pre-cum by the time my mouth found his cock.

Then that clean, sweaty smell of his ass hit my nostrils.

He thought that I was planning to suck his dick, so he was surprised when I licked my way around to his ass. It must have been something that he wanted, however, because as my lips reached the top of his crack, he bent over slightly, giving me greater access to his man cunt. His body was now facing away from me. I pushed my tongue deep inside him, tasting his essence as I ate his ass.

A hot-looking older Latin man appeared out of the shadows, surveying the sex scene unfolding in front of him. He pulled my man's cock out of my hands and began to jerk it as he unzipped his jeans and fished out his own hard dick.

Still clenching his muscular ass-cheeks around my face, my newfound lover grunted to the Latino: "Nice cock, man."

I knew that keeping my tongue in his ass would be the only way to keep this beautiful man all to myself, so I continued reaming his steamy hole.

The Latino made out with my guy while playing with his own dripping cock. Then he took a step back, his dark hard-on throbbing in the moonlight, and took a hit of poppers. My guy bent over to slurp on the Latino's boner and I buried my tongue deeper and deeper, my face straining against my man's hairy crack. Then I grabbed his juicy cock again and jerked him as he sucked cock and I sucked ass.

As my hand grew more accustomed to how my guy liked to have his dick stroked, I was able to pull his cock closer to me so that I could lick it as I continued to tongue fuck his asshole for all that I was worth.

The Latino grabbed my lover's head and spunked into his willing mouth, the excess cock-snot dribbling down his chin. The Latino then put his dripping dick back into his jeans, said "later" and returned to the shadows.

Selfish prick, I thought as I continued to make out with my guy's hairy hole. He seemed to be pushing his ass harder onto my tongue than before. Lost in my lust, I hardly noticed when his spit-slicked hand started jerking my throbbing cock.

"Hey, if you don't let up on my hole," he panted, "I'm gonna cum too soon, man."

By this time I couldn't have stopped even if the police had shown up, so I continued to tongue-fuck him.

"Oh God, you're so deep in my hole, dude. Nobody ever ate my ass so deep before."

I started sucking his cock from behind and playing with his slick hole at the same time. Then, just as I reinserted my tongue into asshole, I felt hot splashes of cum shooting all over me. Some of his cum landed on the dirt, but the majority of his load sprayed my cock, balls and stomach, providing me with additional lube as I jerked my cock.

"What does my ass taste like?" he asked as he pulled me to my feet and kissed me hard. Our cocks rubbed together. His cum glued our bodies together. As we kissed, I could taste the Latin dude's jizz.

Deliberately, my man led me deeper into the woods.

We came to a small, almost secluded clearing. The path had ended. Naked men lined the perimeter trees, searching for partners or just watching the action in the clearing. My man walked over to a beach blanket. In the moonlight, I could barely make out his clothing piled in a corner of the blanket along with several bottles of lube and Rush.

This fucker came prepared, I thought.

We lay naked together on the blanket. Soon, his tongue was as busy in my mouth as mine had been in his ass. He loved to suck face. Amazingly, his cock was still hard, even after the enormous load he had shot on me. He rolled on top of me, kneeling between my legs and playing with my nipples.

Now he wants my ass, I thought, reveling in his touch, prepared to give myself to him. He put his hands behind my head, pulling me closer for yet another soulful kiss. Then gradually, he pulled me up into a sitting position.

Again, we were mouth-to-mouth and cock-to-cock.

He straddled my body and reached across the blanket for the bottle of Rush. His spit-slicked hole rubbed against my cummy cock. I reached up to play with his tits. He moaned as I touched his swollen nipple. His body shook with ecstasy and he started grinding his crack over my pole.

"You ever fuck a guy before?" he asked, unscrewing the bottle.

"Sure," I lied. "Lots of times." I couldn't believe that this hot masculine guy was talking to me about fucking his ass.

"Never wanted one in me before," he said. He slid his ass-crack up and down against my shaft. The feeling was intense. I wanted his hole now!

He took a long hit of Rush and offered me the bottle.

"You really got me going with that pretty mouth of yours eating my ass. And I really dig your cock, man. I want you in me."

I inhaled the vapors, covering the opposite nostril to maximize the intensity of the hit. All sensation began to center in my throbbing cock.

"You are so fucking hot," I said, pulling his lips to mine for yet another sloppy wet kiss. He broke the kiss, spit into the palm of his right hand and applied it to the head of my dick.

"If it isn't spit, it isn't love," he said. Then he straddled my prick, reached around to place my cockhead next to his sphincter and lowered himself onto me. My cock slid easily into his spit-filled velvet channel. My first time inside another man, and it was as perfect as I had ever imagined. I could feel his body shiver as my cock knob glanced off his swollen prostate. I could see the pre-cum leaking out of his cock as my dick pleasured his manhole. I loved this man more than anyone else that I had ever known.

His face, handsome in the moonlight, took on an ethereal glow as he pounded his ass down on my prick. Each thrust seemed to take him further into a trance-like state and my cock deeper and deeper into him. Although his prick was hard and throbbing, he ignored it, rotating and bobbing his hole up and down on my manhood. This guy liked dick as much as I liked ass.

His tempo changed as his orgasm neared, the image of this gorgeous guy literally fucking himself with my cock making me super horny. His asshole seemed to expand and my cock pistoned into him faster and harder. We came at the same instant, me feeling as if my jism was shooting up into his throat and him grinding his ass onto my member to feel as much of my cock inside of him as possible. He shot volleys of cum between our sweaty bellies.

Afterwards, he stood up, exposing his cum filled hole, which was stretched by the pounding. I could actually see my juices inside his man-pussy. I decided to suck my cum out of this beautiful hairy ass. My mouth found his juicy box. I licked my cum out of him as he writhed in ecstasy.

"Fuckin' hot, man," he groaned. The cum gave his man twat a slimy consistency that it hadn't had before, but it was still delicious. After emptying him of my jizz, we settled into each other's arms on his blanket for a serious make-out session, sharing my load as we kissed.

I had never felt as happy and complete as I did at that moment, holding my lover in my arms. He truly belonged to me, and I to him, in the most personal of ways. My seed was deep inside him and his was all over me.

We had possessed each other completely.

"Jim here, nice to meet you," he said suddenly.

Well, maybe *possessed* was too strong a word.

Ass(id) Trip
Sal

Asses, rear ends, behinds, globes, mounds of flesh, hard bubble butts. Squeezable, slappable, pinchable, it doesn't get much better than that. Why do I love asses? Why wouldn't I? I've always been more of an assman than a dickman. Don't get me wrong, I can definitely appreciate a meaty member. But an ass that's regularly worked out and sticks out and is perfectly proportioned to a man's body can't be substituted.

I don't know if it has to do with the fact that I'm a top, but I've always been more interested in checking a guy out from behind than from the front (I wonder if bottom men are more interested in dicks). Anyway, that was what my fantasies were about growing up: being with an incredible-looking, muscular man who had an incredible-looking ass and sliding my cock right up into that cave of eternal bliss. I always wanted to squeeze the hell out of those asses in the

International Male catalogue underwear section, or even one of the hot guys in the soft-core *Playboy* videos.

I didn't masturbate with my hand as a child. I only masturbated by pretending to fuck my bed and bedspreads. To this day, I still continue doing this. I love the movement and the grinding motion, which is why I usually prefer frottage to regular penetration when I'm with a man.

One time, I stared at one guy's ass for who knows how long and it could've gotten me badly hurt or beat up. It was at a Lollapalooza concert in the early Nineties. I was living in Florida and attending the show with eight other people, all of us doing acid. Once inside the gates, three of us decided we would get beers for everyone and we went and stood in the beer line.

After acquiring the beers, everything went hazy.

I immediately lost everyone I was there with. We had made plans to meet on the hour at a certain place if any of us got separated, but at that point I had started my trip and didn't care about anything else but this one guy's ass. I have a tendency to focus on one certain thing when I'm on drugs, especially acid, and from the moment I saw this guy's ass, I couldn't think about doing anything else. Not even finding my friends.

He was by himself, too, which made it a little bit easier to stalk him, which is what I felt like I was doing. If he were with friends or his girlfriend, I probably wouldn't have followed him. Especially if they had seen me. I can't even remember what he looked like from the front. I'm sure he was good-looking, or maybe I wouldn't have pursued him.

Maybe I would've.

It's hard to tell.

It was a hot day, but I'm pretty sure he was wearing jeans. It's weird to look back on that concert now and not remember anything except following around this guy in hopes that I could score with him. I guess that was my motivation.

I followed him for what seemed like hours. I'm not sure when he first saw me, but if he knew I was following him, he would've said something to me.

Wouldn't he have?

I think he was on something too that day. Wherever he went, I followed. If he stopped, I stopped. Finally, he came to this grassy spot by what looked like a lake (though I'm not sure whether or not there *were* any lakes). He sat down on the grass and I sat down about fifteen feet away. I think this is when he had to know I had been following him. As I lay there looking at him very obviously, he must have thought I was psychotic. Or at least gay.

I don't know where I get my courage from when I'm on drugs, but I ended up crawling right over to him on my hands and knees. He saw me approaching but didn't say anything. I didn't say anything to him either. I finally got to him and was just about ready to molest or rape this poor guy (I can't remember if I actually put my hand on his stomach or was just about to), but he got up and started walking again.

With that, you would've thought I had learned my lesson, but I didn't. I immediately started following him again. I was possessed, mesmerized, and high. I had to have this guy. Especially his ass. Through the crowds we went again. I can just imagine what he must have been thinking. But why didn't he just say *fuck off* or *get away from me, faggot?*

He didn't and that's why I continued to follow.

Eventually, he found his friends again and I sort of stood at a close distance staring at him. I could tell that he was pointing me out and telling his friends that this psycho-homo was following him. That's when I woke up and knew it was time to get out of there.

Moral of the story: if you're going to attend an all-day rock concert or similar type of event and you decide you're going to take acid, make sure that you are literally attached to one of your friends. Or else they could find you later getting your you-know-what kicked!

Moon

Lukas Scott

A bright, bright sky. Grey clouds blown recalcitrantly against the purple night by a hoarfrost wind. Bright white sparks of light shone like dust specks in ultra-violet mediated backrooms. Victoriously bright beside them, a waxing moon, reaching its white fullness tonight. Hidden only now and then by the clouds puffed past its luminescence, the moon's bright beams dripped out of the sky. A magical evening, a magical sky.

Beneath it all, the cold city. The evening creeping quickly, cloaking the lonely concrete car parks and tower blocks. The city skyline fast becoming manmade outcrops of concrete and metal, crowding out the sky above. Milky glows from the dark sky above spotted rooftops with off-white ripples.

A lonely night. Magical, maybe, but lonely, definitely. The crowds wandering the streets, busy disappearing from work, consisted of solitary figures stuck into the same picture frame. Cal, separate, apart, alone, fitted in.

The long lane stretched ahead, gray pavement merging with gray wall in the gray light. Cal kept his head down, not daring to look at the figures brushing past him, waifs crashing into his world. Occasional grunts as shoulders collided were the only communication in this bleak landscape, inhabited by aliens so similar they all merged into one mass. Sharp solitary barks from beggars in doorways reminded Cal he had somewhere to go to tonight, some lonely prison that kept the rain out of his hair.

Back to the same ritual of a microwave meal for one, hours stretching ahead to be filled with bootlegged CDs and satellite TV. The same feeble optimism of answer-phone messages and e-mails, beguiling promises of winking lights and web notifications masking junk mails and caller withheld silences. The relentless ritual of waiting for nightmares to savage sleep. Then morning breaking, like the first sodding morning. The whole bloody thing over again.

It had been a bad day, even as bad days go. Even as Cal's days go. Sell, sell, sell. The advertising spaces seemed like chasms he couldn't fill, the cold calls to prospective clients brick walls he couldn't break through. Even the regulars, the only friends he could name, coldly decided budgets were allocated or passed him round offices until they could find someone responsible for buying advertising—all of whom were absent or struck down by some mysterious plague. Cal visualised them with pustulous boils, wretched misers who had made his own day hell.

Was there no end to it all? No break from the monotonous misery? From the hateful, heterogeneous havens to which the smirking, laughing blokes in his office would return? Squeaky clean kiddies screaming daddy's return, elaborate meals prepared by mother's hand, tomorrow's clothes pressed and hung before a night of family entertainment and, for the lucky, soft unlit lovemaking beneath a goose feather quilt. Warm perfumed heaven.

As advertised.

Cal sold it, but never bought.

Car lights flashed in front of him, a trail of blazing white coming toward him and red dots disappearing away from him. It appeared to be an escape, wagons ferrying the desperate to freedom. They were getting out of here. Out of the city, out of this dreadful hole. The hum-drum and predictable.

It happened before he had noticed, before he could fathom any of it at all. There was only movement, a surreal soundless freeze-frame. He hadn't noticed that there was even a pub there before, a quaint black timber-framed front creaking from years of weathering.

Two men leapt out. Clad in striped tribal rugby tops, hair cropped as if for the marines, they stopped in front of Cal, completely oblivious to his presence. As if rehearsed, but entirely spontaneously, the first dark-haired brute dropped his trousers and pants over his thighs in one move. The second-fairer, a leaner build-dropped to his knees behind his mate. Cal couldn't believe his eyes as he watched the fair man bend forward and plant a loving kiss on his mate's behind, as the first man turned his head and looked on. A sigh of ecstasy issued from his lips, as his friend delivered the single loving blow between the cheeks.

Within an instant, he had pulled his trousers up, his mate too standing again, and they'd rushed together back into the pub. No trace of their strange ritual remained, apart from Cal's open mouth and wide eyes. The blood rushing through him continued to pelt round his body, leaving him with a semi-erection and the after-effects of shock.

Cal stood, disbelieving, but certain that what he believed to have happened in front of him really had been so. *One bloke kissing another's arse in the street?* What madness had befallen them? What unheard of insanity! And yet—what touching beauty. What delightful rebellion.

Cal staggered forward. His legs seemed heavy, his mind weighed down with the impossibility of his erotic vision. Men doing *that* in the street?! What was the world coming to? How had he been witness to this?

Cal stopped as he came to the door of the tavern. It seemed ordinary enough, a simple bar menu and drinks list displayed in an alcove sheltering an open door. A familiar whiff of weak lager, cheap whisky and cheaper cigarettes hit him. The smell reminded him of weddings and Christmas parties, merry celebrations lubricated with liquor. It was an inviting smell, offering escape from the woes of the world outside. The temptation was strong, though Cal feigned resistance.

Not for long however. The image in his mind, the laughter echoing from within and the smells and temptations of the bar were all too much for him on this miserable day. A quick half pint, maybe, then he might get on his way. Just whet the whistle, Cal thought.

He crossed the threshold, no one noticing his arrival. The bar was busy, men finishing work and supping a bevie before returning home to hearth and kin. It was all men, a fact so obvious that Cal didn't notice until he had bought his pint ("I asked for a half, I'm sure I did") and sat on a tall wooden stool in the corner of the bar closest to the door. He looked around and saw no feminine presence, even the staff being male. The thought crossed his mind that it might be a gay bar, making him feel a little uneasy, and questioning the sexuality of whoever he happened to be looking at. Which in itself could be a problem, so he tried not to look at anyone in particular.

But no, there was nothing to suggest such a thing. The sports trophies, the saucy postcards from abroad behind the bar, the casualness with which the other men chattered and laughed—there was no cruising here. This was not a bar in which men sought out other men.

And yet there had been the earlier apparition. The two men who had been perversely intimate in front of him on the street. He looked for them now, and saw them with a group of other men, acting as if nothing untoward had happened. As if, only minutes before, they had been clapping each other on the back instead of kissing one another's arse.

Cal looked out of the window. It was frosted, but through the frost he could see a cloud drifting away from the bright moon in the sky. As it separated, revealing the orb in all its glory, Cal felt himself shiver and watched as the room began to luminesce.

He wasn't the only man to notice. Throughout the bar, faces turned toward the eerie light, entranced by the milky glow. In front of him, a young man dropped his trousers, as a tweed-suited gentleman knelt down and kissed the lad's buttocks. Behind the bar, one of the bartenders also shucked off his black trousers as the manager knelt and caressed the tanned toned arse in front of him. The men he had seen earlier partnered again, this time the fair man proffering his anus for a moment or two of tonguing from his colleague. Not just a kiss, this, but a loving tongue roaming between the buttocks, from the base of his colleague's ball-sack to the top of his cheek's cleavage. The chattering, the laughter stopped, as men engaged in anal adoration the likes of which Cal had never seen and could not comprehend.

Dazed by the bizarre couplings, Cal rose and made his way through the ecstatic gropings. He made his way to the other side of the bar, where an open door led to a courtyard. Surely that must offer some escape from this madness, some shortcut back to normality. What had happened to these grown men? He could not, would not remain a passive witness to such acts any longer. The first time had been unbelievable, unimaginable, but this was . . . some form of witchcraft, surely?

A sharp chill struck him as he walked outside onto the stone flags of the beer garden. The area was awash with the cool glow of the moon, a filtered light show playing over the open garden. Night stock filled the air with its sweet balm. Cal had not stepped far before he realised that this was no escape, but a descent into further insanity.

In front of him, six men were grouped together in a circle, kissing and tonguing naked buttocks. Moans issued forth from the writhing mass, interspersed with the joyful smacking of lips against flesh. The men were from many generations, old and young alike, giving each pleasure under the moon's bright stare. He recognised men from his neighbourhood, all of them married to young and beautiful wives, cavorting with each other and touching and kissing each other's backsides. In a corner, kissing a pensioner's wrinkled white arse flesh, Cal recognised his manager, supplicant before the elderly man's anus. The man smiled as the sales manager's tongue probed his puckered hole.

There was no stopping this strange lust. A spell had been cast on all the men assembled in that place, and Cal himself was beginning to fall under the unlikely charm. Trembling, Cal set his pint down on the floor to his right. He began to unbuckle his belt, unzipping his trousers and feeling them tumble round his ankle. His hands slipped underneath the elastic of his jockey shorts, easing them over his thighs and causing them to join the trousers heaped over his shoes. He stood naked from the waist down, looking up at the moon and devoid of all his usual senses. It seemed that he was flying, that he was free and weightless. The warm mouth against his buttocks caused him only pleasure, and as he looked over his shoulder, he looked directly at the handsome young college student who was devoting himself to Cal's anus. The youth planted his first kiss on the left buttock, then another on the right, before following a path of kisses inwards to the very circle of Cal's maleness. Cal shuddered with unknown delight as he felt the wet caress of the young man's tongue probing against his tender sphincter, making him spasm in joy. For the first time in his life, Cal felt truly wanted, truly desired, truly prized. The moment seemed to last forever, but was over in an instant.

As suddenly as it had been liberated, the moon's power was imprisoned anew by an indolent cloud masking its light. Not seeming to realise what had happened between them, the men around Cal began dressing, returning to mundane conversations and bar rituals. The student who had been pleasuring Cal's backside took a seat next to his professor, fiercely remonstrating with his tutor for having given him a poor mark. Cal, alone, seemed to remember what had transpired, remembered the moon's charm.

There was nothing to do but finish the pint and make his way back home, which Cal duly did. Outside again, the world continued as Cal trekked home. Above him, the moon smiled, a beam as bright as any ray of sun. Cal, finding himself still undone, pulled up his zipper and walked on, not daring to look up.

Licked, Slurped, Tongued, Nibbled

Jim

I was in town for business. As usual, I perused the message boards and posted some myself. It's a shame to have a hotel room and no one to share it.

His ad said he was straight but curious and wanted to meet someone who would understand, be gentle and take things slow and easy. When I opened the door at 6:00 a.m., he was better looking than I had dared hope. He was very nervous, having never before done anything with a guy. He said he had discovered some gay porn on the net and realized he found it erotic.

I helped him undress and asked a few questions to determine how far he would go. He would jack me, but no kissing, no sucking (by him) and nothing anal.

Hmm . . . this will be a challenge.

He was 32 and slender, without an ounce of fat. He had a dark complexion with a mischievous smile that made me horny. He was hung like a horse. Even soft, I guess him to be at least 7.5 inches and quite thick. Beautiful low-hangers completed the package.

I had him lay on his back and tongued his balls and shaft. Then I lay back and he pumped me by hand. We tried several positions, including him kneeling on the bed, feeding me his cock. He seemed too nervous to cum.

I had never before eaten ass. Never thought I would. But he smelled so good, so clean, and had such a firm bubble butt. When that boy-ass got in my face, out came my tongue. I was on my back and he was squatting on my face. I licked, slurped, tongued, nibbled. He moaned, wriggled, bucked. We were both surprised. I'd never done it, he'd never had it done.

His monster cock got harder and he began to stroke himself with one hand and my throbbing rod with the other. I ate and ate. In a moment, we both blew loads on my stomach.

I see him most every trip now. Eating ass is now standard procedure. He doesn't eat yet, but he has learned to kiss and suck. Just wait. . . .

Booty and the Beach

Greyson B. Moore

Right after my first year at a small college in the Midwest in the Seventies, I got a job as a lifeguard on a beach at a small lake. I thought it would be a good opportunity to check out some male butt. However, mostly families came to the beach and most of the men had flat or flabby butts, so there wasn't much worth looking at.

Finally, on one extremely hot day in August, there was something to look at. A muscular, middle-aged, 6'8" tall brother walked onto the beach wearing the most incredible swimsuit that I had ever seen. It was a fluorescent orange/pink knit that appeared to glow next to his dark chocolate-colored skin. It looked like two triangles sewed together at the crotch and then tied together on both sides. The back triangle revealed a lot of cleavage. And there was some pretty impressive cleavage. When he sat down on the blanket he brought, the triangle rode up his split and looked almost like a thong.

He got up and proceeded to slather his body, including the exposed parts of his glutes with baby oil. He even stuck his oily hands under the back of his swimsuit a couple of times. The other people on the beach turned their heads nervously away as he continued to sensuously oil himself up. But he didn't care.

He then lay facedown on his blanket, his big beefy buns sticking up in the air looking like the letter M on steroids. Man I wanted on top of them. I looked at his butt as much as I could without being noticed that day. Luckily, as a lifeguard, I had 1940s-style baggy trunks on, so my boner wasn't evident.

When my relief came, I didn't want to leave. But Mr. Booty got up and left so I saw no reason to stay. I took a shower and put on my street clothes and headed for the parking lot. As I was walking toward my car, I heard a deep bass voice say from a van:

"Hey, blood, how long you been workin here?"

It was Mr. Booty.

"Not long." I studied his face and figured he was about fifty. The thought of being hit on by a man that old turned me off. I turned around and started to walk away. I heard him get out of the van and I turned back toward him. He was still wearing the triangles but now he had on a pair of Converse and white crew socks. I snickered a little when I saw the white socks. Typical old man, I thought.

I studied his physique very carefully and admired the fact that he had kept himself in shape, no gut or sagging tits like a lot of men his age. In fact, his pecs were stunningly handsome. I checked out his crotch and noticed there was very little bulge. I was pleased with the fact that I was probably a great deal bigger between the legs than him. I'm no foot-long wonder, but I knew that if I were wearing that suit, there would be a bigger bulge between the legs.

"How 'bout you and I take a walk?" he said rather coyly. He was also carrying a small paper bag. "I've got something I bet you want."

I figured he was a dealer and wanted nothing to do with his scene. "I've got to get home," I said firmly.

"Like I said, boy, I've got something you need." He patted his butt, then briefly undid one of the side ties of his swimsuit, completing exposing a buttcheek. Seeing the lighter color where his suit had been was a real turn-on.

His nerve impressed me. At any moment, he could have been seen by the local police patrol and busted for public indecency.

"What's in the bag?" I asked.

"Just a toy or two. Toys for big boys, that is."

"Show me."

"Not here," he said. "Let's take a walk."

We headed down a small path that led to the woods on the other side of the lake. When we got to a place where we couldn't be seen from the beach or from the parking lot, he opened the bag and revealed the contents: a tube of lubricant and about a half dozen assorted French ticklers.

I'd never seen a tickler before, so I stared at them.

"Satisfied?" he asked, sounding a little insulted. He closed the bag and dropped it on the ground. Before I could answer, he pulled down my pants. "Fine piece of chocolate," he said as he pulled out my meat. "Bet it tastes fine, too." He started to suck on it. I was hard and ready to cum in no time. He sensed it and removed his mouth. "Don't want to get a cavity from the crème filling," he said with a chuckle. "Let's walk some more."

He picked up the bag. I pulled up my pants with some difficulty because of my boner and walked with him. We walked halfway round the lake. The other side had virtually no beach, so no one was there. We stopped at an old picnic table that had definitely seen better days. A lot of brush had grown up around it, so we couldn't be seen from the lake.

"Put this on," he said, throwing me a tickler. "I like the feeling." Because the tickler looked essentially like a condom, I knew what to do with it. I pulled down my pants and briefs and nervously unrolled it over my stiffy. This was my first time doing the backdoor boogie, but I figured he had done it many times. I was afraid my virginity would show, so I tried to act nonchalant.

The tickler was red and covered with bumps of all shapes and sizes. The end had all of these little feelers on it and a reservoir. I looked down at my sheathed dong and it looked really weird. In fact, I thought it looked ugly. The tickler was also making my dong sweat profusely, which made the tickler feel like it was going to slide off at any minute.

"Ready to get a piece?" he asked, then turned around toward the picnic table and pulled down the seat of his swimsuit, revealing the top of his buns. Right away, he pulled them up, then pulled them down again, exposing just a little more. He was teasing me. He pulled them back up, then pulled the triangle together so that it looked like a thong. "Like my butt-floss?" he asked. I juiced into the tickler when I saw that.

"Glad to see you appreciate a fine set of male buns," he said with a chuckle. "Bet you can get hard again right away and I bet I know just the thing to do it." He bent over the top of the table and stuck his butt in the air. A shaft of sunlight hit it, emphasizing it.

I couldn't believe this was happening.

He undid both sides of his swimsuit and pulled down the back. His big firm butt was now completely exposed. His buns were massive. Talk about having a bubble butt. This guy had a hot-air-balloon butt. I wondered how he ever found pants to fit over them. I figured he had to buy them several sizes too big so that he could even pull them up over his ass. His cheeks were perfectly smooth and hairless and had the hottest tan lines. Where the swimsuit had been was a lighter shade of brown in the shape of a triangle. It seemed to point to his butthole. Looking at it made me even hotter.

"Now that you're hard," he said, parting his cheeks, "why don't you put that banana in my split?"

His rosebud was tiny and there wasn't a single hair

around it. I was stunned at the nakedness of it. I was also shocked that a man that had probably been butt-balled hundreds of times could have a hole so small.

"Let me show you the way." He squirted a generous amount of lube on his finger, then shoved his greasy digit into his hole. "Cleaned it this morning," he said. "And it's still clean. Now come on, boy, screw my hole like you want. It won't bite. Shoot, when I was your age, I spurted everywhere I was allowed."

I was shaking with lust. I thought I was going to have a heart attack. I wanted it bad, but I didn't know if I should.

"Come on, boy, you won't burn for helping a man out. And you would be doing me a favor because I need it. All I got at home is some ugly pink rubber dicks and they don't feel as good as a real piece of chocolate." He kept on coaxing me until I felt like I had no choice.

I was surprised how easily I went into him. His greedy hole sucked my dick head in, but because of the massive size of his buns and the position he was in, I couldn't push my dick in as far as I wanted. I wanted to be in him up to my balls, but I could only get partially in. I asked him to turn over, but he wouldn't. "I like it doing it the way doggies do," he said with an enormous grin on his face.

I had to make do and thrust halfway in and out. I bent over as I thrust, which gave me a good look at the back of his head. I could clearly see that he had a bald spot.

I'm screwing a man almost as old as my grandpa, I thought for a moment.

I stood back up so that I could look down at the buns I was thrusting in and out of. I quickly forgot about how old Mr. Booty was.

The tickler, which was filled with semen and sweat, dulled the sensation. "That's the way I like it, boy," he said. "Fill that black butt up. Pound it real good. Help a brother out." I found his talking while we screwed a turn-on and an annoyance. I figured if that I was doing it good enough, he shouldn't be talking so much.

But he kept talking and I kept thrusting until I finally shot. I thought I was going to die because I was sweating so much and breathing so hard. Even doing wind sprints up and down hills didn't make me breathe so hard.

When it started hurting to be inside of him, I pulled out. The semen and sweat filled tickler stayed behind though. His greedy butthole clenched it so tightly, my dick slid right out of it.

When he felt me out of him, he pulled up the seat of his swimsuit and tied it back up. I wondered if he knew that I had left the tickler in his butt.

"I see you left a little something to remember you by," he said. "Sure beats a Hallmark. Thanks for helping a brother out. Best I've had yet."

He grabbed his paper bag and walked away. I looked at his butt and noticed a spot spreading over the back of his swimsuit. I wondered who he was, where he came from, and whether I would ever see him again.

I never saw him again and I never found out who he

was. I also sometimes wonder if I will ever see booty like that again. I have seen a few that came real close, but I will keep on looking for another one just as perfect, no matter how long it takes.

Butts and Holes

Docjack

This is my story of how I came to love and enjoy eating butt.

I'm a late bloomer. I lived a straight life for 32 years, then a bisexual but totally compartmentalized life for another 20. Finally now, I've lived for 11 years as a gay man with a gay life, but I'm still in a mixed orientation marriage. It has been difficult for my lover, my wife and me.

My introduction to butt was most inauspicious. It occurred because I wanted cock to suck. In a small, semi-rural town in the Seventies, sucking cock was not easy, especially because I was so deep in the closet, denying my gayness even to myself. One day in a tearoom, I met a guy named Rich, who let me suck him, but only if I ate his hole. I overcame my inhibitions and found that I could eat his ass and that it was okay. I did it twice, and in a couple of weeks, I had a horrible case of hepatitis and felt like I was dying. That was enough to make me steer clear of butt for a long time.

Then I saw Rich again. We started meeting at the tea-room, then going to my office for sex. He had a really nice eight-inch cock that was a real treasure. It was really thick—too thick for a near virgin to take up the ass comfortably—but it really filled my mouth up and was very satisfying to suck. His cum was a taste treat. Rich made it clear that what he liked best was fucking ass and having his hole eaten, and if I wanted to suck his cock, I needed to get fucked or eat his hole. Finding guys to suck him was easy because he had such a fine specimen. Finding guys to fuck was only slightly more difficult for the same reason. Yet getting guys to rim, kiss and tongue his hole was hard where we lived. So he told me: if I took care of his need for head for his hole, he would share his cock with me.

Since I didn't want to lose my chance to enjoy his eight inches repeatedly, I agreed to eat his butt. Rich would get so excited when I'd kiss, lick, suck and probe his hole with my tongue. His being turned on turned me on. I really found that eating butt was great fun. It got so that I would spend almost all our time together eating his butthole. He was squeaky clean and I found the lips of his asshole much more interesting and satisfying than the lips of any mouth. His hole was aesthetically imperfect, but as a sex organ, it was made for oral sex. It responded so actively, even passionately to my lips and tongue, puckering and kissing me back or relaxing to allow my tongue to probe and penetrate. He was doing me as much or more than I was doing him. I found that I could eat ass for hours and not tire of it if my partner enjoyed it. And Rich really enjoyed having me eat his hole. Pleasing my partner was key to my enjoyment. Our sessions became almost exclusively about eating butt with just brief lip service to his cock at the beginning and end of a session.

Like me, Rich was married with kids. It was hard to find time to get together and he was afraid of getting into a relationship. We had to cross paths at the tearoom in order to meet and have our fun. Eventually, we drifted apart. Rich's legacy to me was teaching me the joys of eating a manhole. I am deeply indebted to him for enabling me to enjoy this.

I met Matt at my mall tearoom when he was only 16. We were both cruising for sex. It was wonderful. Our first sex was my giving him a quickie blowjob with my head under the stall divider. His cum that day was the sweetest I've ever had the privilege of tasting. We started meeting regularly and I worried about the legality of it; but he wanted it and I couldn't refuse him (to this day, anything Matt wants, Matt gets from me).

I wanted to do something "special" for Matt, and the most special thing I could think of was rimming him. For several months he refused. Finally, he allowed me to do him. The first time I ate his asshole was the most perfect sexual experience I've ever had. Matt was essentially hairless except for his carrot-colored bush. His butt was a wonder to behold, muscular and smooth, the classic bubble butt. His hole was perfection. No blemishes. No hemorrhoids. He would wink it for me. I would dive in and kiss, suck, lick and tongue that rhapsodic hole. And he'd pucker the hole and kiss me back or relax it so my tongue could probe deeper. It was pure heaven. I felt so incredibly close and at one with him when my mouth and his hole made love to each other.

Matt and I have been friends now for 11 years. Our 35 year age difference is too great an obstacle to becoming life partners—something I regret, for I am in love with him. Eating his ass that first time made me fall hopelessly in love with him. We remain very special friends with a very special relationship. When he is not in a relationship with someone, he will still thrill me on occasion by making love to me. I've sucked his cock on many occasions and thrilled to his fucking my ass probably 50 or so times. But the greatest treat is when I get to eat his perfect hole. That's happened only five or six times in 11 years, and every time, it has been an exquisite, mind-blowing experience for me. I feel totally at one with him.

He is very clean, but once there was the tiniest bit of shit there. I lapped it up and since it was Matt's shit, I savored it and ate it. I know that sounds gross, but it really wasn't. I always thought I would hate the taste of shit. It wasn't bad, and because it was Matt's, there was nothing else to do but swallow it. I wanted it inside me just like I want his cum inside me and would gladly drink his piss if he ever cared to share it.

He's in a relationship now, so his gorgeous body is off

limits. But if that relationship ends, I know I will get invited to kiss and eat his hole again. Meanwhile, I settle for fantasizing about it. The fantasies include my eating his hole to prepare it for his lover, then licking it clean after his lover has shot his load and feltching his lover's cum from it. I've told him I'm even willing to try to become his asswipe and clean his hole after he's taken a dump. I have no idea if I could actually do that. Yes, I've eaten a tiny piece of shit, but I realize that a really dirty hole might be quite different, even if it's shit from the young god I worship. In fantasy, we can do anything and it remains clean and safe.

It's fun to have these hot raunchy fantasies. I've shared some of them with Matt and he has enjoyed them. I've fantasized many times about being invited to eat his hole and finding it dirty, then being told that the only way Matt's lover will allow Matt to offer me his hole is if I lick it clean. I want to eat Matt's hole so much that I wouldn't hesitate to do it, no matter how shitty it was. I've never been into scat, but even having him shit on me sounds alluring if it includes eating his hole clean. It's not eating shit that is the attraction. It's his perfect ass and hole and the intense closeness, even oneness, that I experience when my lips lock onto the lips of his asshole. I've even fantasized about eating his hole and opening it up with my mouth so he shits some in my mouth and the shit becomes the equivalent of cum in our interaction.

Matt has read my fantasies about my being his subservient raunchy bottom, ready to attempt to drink his hot piss right from his spigot and lick his hole clean after a dump. I worried that these raunchy fantasies would turn him off, but the fear didn't keep me from sharing them. He reassures me that he enjoys them and tells me not to be afraid to share them with him. Yet I've kept private the feltching fantasy and the fantasy of having him shit on me or in my mouth. In spite of his reassurance, I'm afraid to tell him. Paradoxically, it is the extremely transgressive and submissive nature of the fantasy that makes me hope he would agree to do this while still in a relationship with his lover.

My freedom to have such fantasies came from reading. I learned about feltching from that great gay classic, *Faggots* by Larry Kramer. Another book called *Meat,* an anthology of gay men's wilder experiences, included several stories involving scat and I found myself turned on by these stories to the point of having to jerk off after reading them. Further exploration led to a zine called *BTF* (Butt to Face). In it were personal ads, including one that was a real turn-on for me:

TOP WANTS RAUNCHY RIMMERS
Hot, handsome, 41 y/o, bearded, leather top, HIV neg-, 5'5", 130#, solid dark hair, blue eyes, very hairy chest, legs and ass, 6" uncut, seeks hungry, submissive bottoms who would enjoy smelling and licking clean my unwashed or unwiped asshole. After my morning shit, you get one wipe with the tissue. Then I'll squat over your face, bare butt in black leather chaps, and your mouth, lips and tongue will lick and suck clean the rest.

I jacked off to that ad countless times, imagining that I would be that raunchy rimmer. I finally got up the courage to answer the ad, but because I had no experience in leather, he dissuaded me from making the three-hour trip to service him. Time passed and I kept re-reading that ad and keep getting turned on by it.

I've written some letters to him but never attempted to send them. Now, I no longer have his address or telephone number. I have also written to the zine in hopes that it still exists, but so far, all the letters remain unsent. Now, I want to share a letter I wrote to him:

Hi. If you are reading this letter, it means a lot of obstacles have been overcome, and that it is my destiny to meet you and for my mouth, lips and tongue to be your asswipe for a day or weekend or week. I know from our one telephone conversation that part of your enjoyment in being rimmed is the thrill you get from having someone eat your shit. So if this letter and the earlier ones I wrote and never had the nerve to send until now finally get to you, I hope you will not try again to dissuade me, but rather accept that it is our destiny to meet. You are a teacher. Teach me and I will eat your dirty, smelly, shitty hole clean exactly the way you like.

We never met because I had no experience in leather. I am not into pain or bondage. I am into pleasing and I really think I can be the raunchy, submissive, hungry rimmer you want. I've eaten dirty holes before but never an unwiped one. You are a teacher by profession. With your help and encouragement, I know I can clean your hole with my mouth. That may be as far as we can go. My hope and fantasy is that you will be able to bring me to the point where you will be shitting into my mouth and I eat your shit right out of your hole. I know that is a lot to be able to do. I may freak out and not be able to do it. I know enough about you to know that that is something you would enjoy. You made it clear that having someone eat your shit is the whole point of letting someone eat your ass. Raunchy rimmers are probably not all that rare, but I am willing, not only to learn how to do that, but also to learn to eat the shit directly from your butthole.

I've been educated by reading a lot and I know that real people do eat shit. Yet my hope is that you've never had a shit-eater and the possibility of this happening will make you interested. And even if this is not new, I hope that it is sufficiently rare that the potential of having one of your rimmers "go all the way" and eat your shit right from your hole will make you want to teach and mentor me.

Somehow I can't escape the belief that it is my destiny and yours for me to be your asswipe with my mouth. I am into pleasing. I want to please you. Give me a chance to pleasure you by eating your shit directly from your hole. Give me a chance to be that raunchy, bottom rimmer. I will service you as a fully submissive bottom. My goal is to be the best raunchy rimmer you've ever experienced. Please give me that chance.

If invited for a visit, I will be a total submissive bottom. Pain and bondage are out, but I'm open to trying anything else. I'm 62, yet I am inexperienced. It was that lack of experience that made you discourage me from trying to meet you.

Offsetting my age and inexperience is my eagerness to succeed in acting out this raunchy fantasy with you. So please, this time, encourage rather than discourage me from trying. The fact that 5 or 6 years have passed since our first and only conversation speaks worlds about my fears and inhibitions.

That this whole scene still remains my hottest fantasy says much about its power in my life. I've thought of offering you a money guarantee if I fail to eat your ass clean after your morning shit. I've thought of offering a small tuition to compensate you for the time spent teaching me how to best service your butthole. I want you to know that this is a sincere offer and I really want you to give me a chance to experience your hot hole with my hot, talented, eager, hungry, submissive mouth.

Republican City Dam

Donny Smith

In spite of what you might've heard, it is possible to keep a secret in a small town.

I don't have sex here, of course. For that, there's a few places where the truckers stop their rigs along Highway 36 in Kansas, and the rest stops on I-80. And for gay life, there's a bar in Kearney, and one in Grand Island. I don't need much. And people remember that I dated some girls in high school, and even after. They don't seem to have much interest in my personal life. I'm just one of those life-long bachelors.

I like it here. I manage my mom and dad's cafe about half a mile from the dam. Officially it's the Harlan County Reservoir, run by Nebraska Public Power and the Army Corps of Engineers. During the year the local farmers keep us open, barely, and in the summer we do our real business. All those fishermen and water-skiers and off-sale beer. On Mondays in summer, I can go out on the lake. And I'm not a great hunter, but I love the canyons and bottomlands in the fall.

One Saturday morning in May, this kid comes in to apply for a summer job. The son of my parents' next-door neighbors, back from the university. One of those small-town athletes. High school basketball star. A big fish in a little pond. Kind of a clown. But didn't lose his cockiness at college. And didn't gain the "freshman twenty" either. I'd seen him just a day or two before, mowing his parents' lawn in nothing but the satin shorts from his old basketball uniform. His ass was two perfect blocks of flesh. And I think the first thing he said as he handed me his paperwork was, "Like what you see?"

I hired him on the spot.

He got attentive training. I couldn't help it: whenever we worked together, I made sure to stand behind him. I wouldn't give him the apron we normally wear in the kitchen. Hides too much. Sometimes I'd give him a job, then just stand and stare. A few times he caught me with my mouth open.

Not a bad worker. But he'd make comments. He'd wait till I was bent over picking something up off the floor, then he'd look at my butt and say, loud enough for a few customers to hear: "How's he gonna keep me down on the farm when he lets himself go like that?" Then he'd give me that grin that made my crotch tingle. But really I should've found an excuse to lay him off. I didn't need any temptations in my hometown. Besides, I haven't let myself go. I still get carded at bars.

I once read an article in *Reader's Digest* about lucid dreaming. It's those moments in a dream when you realize that you're dreaming. Usually you wake up right away, but if you can stay asleep and focus your thoughts, you can do whatever you want. It takes practice, but you take control of your waking life by taking control of your dreams. Each night, I concentrated on his image as I drifted off. The idea was that then I would dream about him, and there at least, I'd touch him. My right hand would move down his back as we kissed. One finger would trace the crack down to where it puckered. My left hand would slide down his belly. One finger would touch the tip of his cock, stroking the slit. Till it exploded. But all summer long I hardly slept. Rubbed myself raw. Nothing but frustrating dreams. . . .

It's late August. I'm in the back room rotating stock with him. I step into the little broom-closet toilet for a minute to take a piss. When I open the door, he has the three-foot stepladder in the doorway and is shifting stuff around in the cubbyhole above the closet. But thing is, he has his fly partly undone, and I can see the outline of his dick in his jeans pointing up toward his right front pocket. He's standing on the top step of the ladder.

"Hey, that's not safe!" I say.

"Well, if you'd grab hold, I wouldn't fall."

I'm careful, but have to play along: "I wouldn't know where to put my hands."

He scratches his belly, then sticks his hand down his pants to scratch his balls. "Well, you could figure something out." And he pushes his hand forward, unzipping his jeans all the way.

More than I hoped for. I reach up and put my fingers gently on his underpants where they cover his cockhead. A little wet spot is already there. I rub it with one finger till it spreads over the entire head. His dick shows hot pink and purple through the white cloth. He's clutching hard at the doorframe and thrusting toward my mouth. "Go ahead," he says.

I put my hands on his hips and push his underpants and jeans down to his knees. I can just reach his balls with my tongue. They jerk away from me at every touch. He bends his knees and his dick hits my nostrils. Then his flesh slips into my mouth. He lets out a long, loud groan, and lets go of the sill. As he starts to fall backward, I catch hold of his ass. He twitches and jerks, but he's not coming yet.

He stands there panting and holding my head. His ass is everything I imagined. Tense and cold like marble, slippery now with sweat. Where I'm standing the yeasty smell of his crotch mixes with the sharp smell of his underpants. His dick subsides a little and rests on my hair. I pull him down a bit and let his dick slide down to my forehead, then to my nose, then to my lower lip. I gulp it in to the base and start nibbling at his balls. He has to hold on tight to my hair. He's hard again and thrusting. Then he says, "Suck it."

Something makes me want to stop. I don't like the tone of his voice.

I pull away and duck between him and the doorframe, and I lay hold of his thighs from behind him.

He tries to turn—"Hey, what are you doing?"—but can't really, on his perch with his pants around his knees. But he's at the perfect height now. His full fragrance hits me. "I don't want you to," he says. I try to lick the crease where his right cheek joins his thigh. He squirms away. I pull him back. I run my tongue up along the cheek toward his crack, savoring the salt and that taste that's more like a smell. He isn't so much squirming as shaking now. I run my tongue down now, till I find hair, then press in deep. He clenches hard. I lick my thumb and use it to circle his tightness, moving in again. My tongue follows. I match every dodge of his hips, till I find the center. As I force my tongue inside him, my hand reaches around and grabs his dick. Suddenly he grinds his ass back into my face. I hear two or three big splats on the floor and feel hot cum run down my hand and arm. I smear my slimy hand across his belly, then wipe each finger on his jeans.

Finally he speaks: "Shouldn't you have been using a rubber or something?"

Shit. "You mean a dental dam."

"Whatever. Maybe next time."

Gluteus Gluttony

Vernon Maulsby

I love the way he walks, the way his cute butt seems to have its own force field around it, just above the skin, so that the coarsest denim flows like silk when he puts it on. He has the cheeks of a teenager and he'll never see forty again. He knows how good he looks, understands and even welcomes the way his lodestone cheeks draw my hands to them.

The nights are the best. He used to wear underwear to bed, but eventually gave up after a silent war of attrition. I used to burn every pair I found in the laundry hamper. I feigned innocence; he chose not to ask. He knew, I knew he knew; yet it was the unspoken that kept us together for so long.

He has hair on his butt, a fine dusting of short, almost invisible fuzz. It's even all over his cheeks, even in the crease between them, where one usually expects longer hairs. I spend hours exploring the geography of his cheeks, covering the area visually at first, then following up with my hands, free to stray far and wide, but always returning to his flawless cheeks. I discovered a secret thing: the dimple just above the cleft of his buttocks only appears when he is truly aroused. This reaction occurs quickly when my hands or lips touch the cheeks.

Yes, I said lips. My mouth and tongue have carte blanche to travel all over his body, as his mouth and tongue do on my body. I have no reservations about tonguing his cheeks and the cleft between. He loves my attentions as much as I enjoy offering them. He'll relax on his belly and purr like a cat while I love his downy cheeks. I love prolonging the play, watching his attempts to shift his engorging phallus into a more comfortable position without disturbing me and the concert of my hands, lips, and tongue. I've been asked, "What does he taste like?" The inference being that I'm some sort of expert or something.

All I can say is that he tastes like the man I love.

I rarely bother with all of that breeder nonsense of covering his butt with whipped cream, chocolate syrup or the like; he tastes just fine on his own. I do admit to enjoying putting honey on his ass. It's not just the taste. It's the whole process. I can make a style of foreplay just around the sensations found in letting honey slowly drip in a thin line on his waiting cheeks. Art and eroticism become one, when the slowly created drawing warms and adds movements of its own to your designs. The results are always good enough to eat. It is a feast for the eyes and tongue, an exploration to not miss a single bit, a thinly veiled excuse to delve deep into clefts and playfully rummage around the back of his testicles.

All in the name of honey retrieval, you understand.

Penetrating his buttocks is also a joy. The passion makes his passage several degrees hotter than one would expect, as if a fever suffuses his body. We fit together like well crafted spoons. Loving him, loving with him, is like being held within a third loving and dexterous hand. Afterwards, we sleep as we loved, his lovely buttocks against me.

He knows how I feel about his butt and its affect on me. He has a habit of sitting in my lap when we go to parties. My phallus then rises to attention as my mind thinks about the lovely treasure pressed up against me, hidden by clothing. It never fails to amuse him or fill me with chagrin when I then have to rise to greet someone.

Another trick he pulls is wearing something tight and thin, then "accidentally" getting them wet. He knows how wet cloth clings to the globes of his butt and their effect on me.

We shaved his butt once. It wasn't a big deal physically. All he had was a dusting of fuzz anyway. But what turned us on was the ersatz feeling of danger from the use of a razor. It was a turn-on, that one time, like making love in a new location on the globe.

Now you know the reason for my gluteus gluttony.

A Straight Man Who Admires Other Men's Butts

Edward Finley

You may not know this from the tone of this essay, but I'm a straight man. A straight man who admires other men's butts.

"Oh, sure," you may say, "another closeted homosexual."

Say what you will. I am straight and I could write volumes about the beauty of the opposite sex. I love women foremost, but like many straight men, I fantasize about other men's asses. Call me bi-curious. I have not partaken, though, at least not yet.

I have a whole collection of photos of men and their beautiful backsides. I search the Internet for juicy photos. I like all kinds of asses, but most of all, I prefer big, beefy ones with lots of hair, especially around soft, pink anuses. I like the juxtaposition of a tough, hairy ass with a silky, pink hole. It's almost an irony of manhood. This is the one spot where a man is truly vulnerable. Everyone breaks down from the touch of a tongue on his asshole. It's as if your protective cheeks have been gotten through, and your vulnerable spot has been exposed.

I play with my own ass all the time. In bed, it is often the first thing I touch upon waking. I like to spread it. I like to tickle my hole, touching it very softly. I bend over before the mirror and spread my moderately hairy cheeks, admiring my pink hole in all its glory. It's a beautiful, earthy, manly hole. It's fringed by black hair. And it's a friendly hole, loving the touch of a gentle, probing tongue and the buzzing caress of my vibrator.

On other men, sometimes it is the buns themselves I crave. Sometimes tight and muscular, sometimes fleshy and soft. I long to hold them in my hands and soak up their maleness. Other times, it is the crack, that sweaty valley lined with hair that will (someday, I hope) tickle my hands and nose. Still other times, it is the actual hole that I lust for, hidden so snugly and guarded so tightly, just waiting to be entered by my tongue and maybe even my cock.

Which brings me to the matter of cocks. And the rest of the man as well. I like a nice cock: pink, spongy, and bouncy. Of any size. And I can admire a man. But I have no attraction to men. I never have. I lose interest in them as people. What I like is the raw animal nature of a male ass. Not a shaved one but a natural one. There is nothing else in the world like it.

I know there are others like me. Men who prefer women, but who like to look at men and men's asses. Who doesn't like to admire? Women do, so why can't we? I notice everything about the other men in locker rooms—how muscled the chest, how well hung the penis, how well shaped the ass. If I stand in just the right places, I can take advantage of the mirrors so that I can see naked men without them seeing me.

But it's so much more than admiring. So many of us long to run our hands over a well-sculpted male posterior. Or better yet, to plunge our cocks into one. If you could wire us up to a mind-reading machine, what you would hear from us would be shocking (then again, maybe you already know what we are thinking). How much less neurotic would our gender be if we could just admire each other's beauty without shame, like women do?

I first became aware of my ass fetish in—where else?—a locker room. I was seated on a bench when another young man came from the shower to his locker, which was near mine. Out of the corner of my eye, I watched him dry off. At one point, his ass was almost in my face. I couldn't believe it, but it gave me a warm, tingly feeling. I wanted so much to touch the beautiful thing, to run my hands over it, to hug it and kiss it. To this day, I imagine what would have happened if he had let me do that.

Why haven't I indulged yet, you ask? I've had opportunities. I've been hit on at a gay bar when my girlfriend took me. I could've taken a guy home and lived out my fantasy. I once received a love note from a guy in my apartment building. I've been hit on by another guy on the job. But there's disease to worry about, as well as the possibility that he will want something more than just a fling. No, what I need is another guy like me, who doesn't want a relationship, who just wants to get together to explore a mutual fetish.

Playing with my own ass only takes me so far. Fucking it with my vibrator only does so much. I must have another ass to touch, lick and fuck. When I finally do have one, I hope it will be a strong, hairy ass. Big and muscular. Big enough to be a pillow. I want to sleep on it and have sweet dreams. But before that, I want to run my hands over every inch of it. I want to open it up slowly, taking in every nuance of the skin, the crack, and the hair of the half-moons. I want to feel my heart beating wildly and my cock throbbing uncontrollably as I catch my first glimpse of that soft, pink hole.

There, dear readers, is my ass fetish. I wish all of you were lined up in front of me, bent over with your rear ends in my face. Some smooth, some hairy, some tight, some fleshy. I would be on my knees, opening you up, one by one, and having my way with you. After that, you could do whatever you wanted with me.

Any takers?

Ode to Peaches

Chris Veldhoven

The Shepherd and his Dairy Queane,
Two men, both met in field of greene
To drink as one in Summer's sheen
From Passion's honeyed still.

The Queane, Da-rryl, had brought dessert
His pride of shape and fuzz overt
The Shepherd's gaze could not avert
All his senses stood alert
His hunger to fulfill.

The Shepherd in his hands encased
The peach Da-rryl had brought to taste
And with each kiss its down did baste
Then with his tongue its curves retraced
A morsel not was he to waste
This culinary thrill.

Among the peach appeared a rose
From whence it came God only knows
This sweet desert to curl their toes
This garnish for their passion's throes
They quickly ripped off all their clothes
For peaches of Da-rryl!

The Shepherd took his Dairy Queane
And plucked the rose before unseen
And to the peach he added cream
The shear delight made both to scream
"Oh Peaches!", even still.

About the Buttmen

JASON A. ANDRESEN is my pen name. I'm a butt lover of long standing. For me, there are few sights quite as beautiful as the naked male butt. As you may guess, I am quite gay. I live in northern California with my soul mate of seventeen years. "Jim's Butt" is based, in large part, on an actual occurrence in my teenage years. I have published other stories, which can be found at www.rdrop.com/users/mmsa/index.html

JAMIE ANDERSON is an aging computer engineer but is young at heart. Locked in the same skull is a vivid imagination, a weird sense of humor and a filthy mind. He is also an irregular contributor to the *Nifty Archive*.

ALAN BELL *(editor)* took his first editing credit on his junior high school newspaper. Since then, he has edited *Gaysweek,* New York's first lesbian and gay weekly newspaper; *Kujisource,* a black AIDS newsletter; and several magazines for the black lesbian and gay community, most notably *BLK* and *Blackfire.* For six years, he was film critic for the *Los Angeles Sentinel,* a mainstream black weekly. His film criticism has also appeared in the *Los Angeles Times.* Wearing a somewhat different hat, he founded Black Jack, the first commercial black sex and social party club. Alan is a graduate of UCLA, the University of the State of New York and is ABD in sociology at New York University.

ADAM BEN-HUR. "A Flame of Flesh . . . for Eric" was written immediately after our first tender time together with hardly a word or
phrase changed since then. Although I have ideas for "fiction" stories
of love and sex between men, so far it's the real events of my life, written from the truth of my own skin, that have materialized on the page.
If you enjoyed this story, I would appreciate hearing from you. Please
feel free to write to me at adambenhur@yahoo.com

HARRY DAVIS was born in Los Angeles and has spent most of his life
in California. Although educated as an historian, he has devoted most
of his energy to writing of fiction and is presently at work on a novel
satirizing the San Francisco design scene of the 1990s. He divides his
time between San Francisco and Palm Springs.

JAY OLIVER DICKINGSON. "I am a dreamer, a lover, a teller of tales.
I am the dream spinner. I can be anything I want and anything you
want me to be." Presently, he is living in a little house on the prairie in
Southeastern Alberta, Canada, dreaming of a temple of young men
eager for him to worship their butts with his tongue. Previous work
published: "Adidas Feet" in *Quickies 2.*

DOCJACK lives and practices medicine in eastern Pennsylvania. This
is his first published work. He is an opera, theatre and movie queen.
He rides his bicycle to raise money for services for PWAs.

DONMIKA is a 21-year-old, black male from North Carolina. A
sophomore English major, he aspires to be a famous writer one day
and has several erotic black stories on the net at www.Blackmen.com.

BEAU FESSES hangs out in pretentious cafes where he writes steamy
love-poetry, sips over-priced lattes and says hello to anyone who looks
his way. He is subject to sudden spasms of unrequited lust and has
been known to fall for men seen in the windows of passing trains or
on elevators just before the door closes. He has published in other gay
anthologies and would be delighted to hear from readers at beaufesses
@hotmail.com.

EDWARD FINLEY lives in Madison, Wisconsin, where he writes and edits for a living, and where he practices his craft of butt admiration. In locker rooms, on the beach, on the Internet, and in his dirty magazines, he is forever admiring the posteriors of his own sex. As his entry in *Buttmen* attests, he is eager to make his dreams come true someday.

JAMES FRANCIS was born to a blue-collar Italian family and could have missed out on gay life during the hedonistic '70s (despite an early and insistent puberty) had he not discovered the busiest gay cruising area in the Northeast several blocks from his home. The scope and tenacity of his sexual exploits from then on can only be regarded as legendary. Pursuing his romantic life with the common sense and good judgment inherent in any 15 year old has rendered him something of an expert on matters homosexual.

JAMES EARL HARDY is the author of the best-selling novels *B-Boy Blues* (1994), praised as the first gay Africentric hip hop love story; its sequel, *2nd Time Around* (1996); and *If Only For One Nite* (1997). The newest and fourth title in the series is *The Day Eazy-E Died*. He's also penned the biographies *Spike Lee* (1995) and *Boyz II Men* (1996). A 1993 honors graduate of the Columbia University School of Journalism, his byline as a feature writer and cultural critic has appeared in *Entertainment Weekly, Essence, Newsweek, OUT, The Source, VIBE,* and *The Washington Post.* He lives in New York City.

JIM is one of the silent army of closeted married men who has chosen family over self. Whenever possible, he enjoys discreet, safe and sane recreation with like-minded men. He gently encourages his straight friends to be sensitive to gay issues. He is grateful for his many gay friends who respect his choice and the discretion that choice requires. He is a manager in the computer industry and lives in Atlanta with his wife and children.

LASZLO'S TOP FAN. I have written several academic works and two novels, and live in the UK. What qualifies me as a buttman is that I

have been scrupulously attentive to the male rear view since I saw my
first bare bottom at the age of about four. This was when my father
slipped off his underpants and pulled on his pajamas. I'll leave it to
psychoanalysis to argue the significance of this sighting.

BRYCE MARR. Born in Australia, 1969, bi-sexual. Into Rugby League
and Rowing. Really gets off on rimming, male and female. Is always
pleased to meet up with other rugged muscle dudes who like the feel
of a tongue licking out their assholes. Contact: rimmingstud
@hotmail.com

VERNON MAULSBY is a mid-forties, black, gay/TS, Wiccan writer.

GREYSON B. MOORE. My first recollection of being excited by the
male posterior was during *Star Trek* in the '60s when quite young
Captain Kirk was wearing black tights and the lines of his underwear
and the cleavage of his buns could be clearly seen when he bent over.
This excited me. From then on, men's backsides have fascinated me.
Once I saw them without a cover and found out what could be done
with them, I became a full, dues-paying member of the male butt-
lovers club.

STEVE NUGENT was born in Ireland and now lives in Toronto,
Canada. His book reviews, essays, and literary interviews have appeared in *fab* and *Lambda Book Report*. His short fiction has been
published in the collections *Quickies 2* and *Exhibitions*. He has always
preferred the hind view, and believes that beautiful butts should not
only be gazed upon lovingly, but stared at long and lasciviously.

IAN PARQUES. Born London, England. Aged 41. Still resident in
London. I work for an organization that deals with complaints about
advertising. Live with my partner and soon to buy a house together.
Hobbies: theatre, cinema, holidays in America! Realized I was gay at
age 12, first sexual experience: 14. Haven't looked back since! Sexual
interests vary but rimming always comes tops. This is my first attempt
at an erotic story.

ROBINMAN has been active in writing erotic superhero stories for several years, starting in 1993. His work has generally been seen on "fan-fiction" or "slash" message boards and sites in various places around the Internet. Having been offline for some time, now he's back and eager to write more costumed capers for the reading public.

SAL is originally from a small town in northwestern Pennsylvania and currently resides outside of San Francisco where he works for Falcon Studios. He followed his dreams all the way across the country to pursue a creative career in the entertainment/film industry. He has written two screenplays, several poems, including "Whore" for which he won an award, and is also working on an autobiographical account of his coming out process.

LUKAS SCOTT put the Wild back into the West with his first novel *Hot On The Trail* (Idol, 2000) and his short story "There's More To Love (Than Boy Fucks Girl)," which was e-published in MindCaviar's Valentine anniversary cybermag. He has been a university lecturer, theatre director, bookseller, television and film extra, counselor and safer sex worker. His favorite butt belonged to his Games captain at college. Lukas lives in England and would love to hear from readers at LukasScott@aol.com. "Moon" is based on a true-life event.

SIMON SHEPPARD is the author of *Hotter Than Hell and Other Stories* and the co-editor, with M. Christian, of *Rough Stuff: Tales of Gay Men, Sex, and Power* and the forthcoming *Rough Stuff 2*. His work has appeared in over fifty anthologies, including *The Best American Erotica 2002, 2000,* and *1997,* and nearly every edition of *Best Gay Erotica.* Currently he's hard at work on a nonfiction book, *Kinkorama.* He lives in San Francisco.

MICHAEL SKIFF lives in Los Angeles, "where I work as porn director Mark Jensen. Porn plots have comprised that bulk of my writing recently. You know, that stuff you fast forward through. I also have a short story 'Blood Brothers' published in the gay anthology *HIS 3.* I'm grateful that Boo lives on in print."

DONNY SMITH grew up in rural Nebraska (but not in Republican City). He now works at Swarthmore College and puts out the zine *Dwan*. His poems, translations, and articles have appeared in many magazines in the United States and Argentina, including *Holy Titclamps*, *James White Review*, *Evergreen Chronicles*, and *Big Bang*.

TROY YGNACIO SORIANO originally conceived of "America's Passion Kings" as a fantasy tribute of sorts to an early favorite writer of his, Jean Genet. Among other writing projects, he is also completing a first novel, *All Points Meet Here*. He lives in Boston, Massachusetts. He maintains a website at www.troysoriano.com.

JAY STARRE was raised in California and emigrated to British Columbia as a teenager. He currently writes gay erotic fiction for various magazines and anthologies, including *Honcho*, *Torso*, *Mandate*, *International Leatherman*, *Bear*, *Friction 4*, *Rentboys* and *Skinflicks 2*.

THE BGM POET is 27 years old and currently working on his AA degree in Maryland. His poems, including "AIDS in my Eyes," have been published by the Famous Poet Society in Los Angeles, the International Library of Poetry in Owings Mills, Maryland, as well as in other publications. BGM is a buttman because he enjoys the beauty, feel, texture and joy that booty brings to a same gender loving man such as himself.

CHRIS VELDHOVEN descends from a long line of queer folk. He supports his "lavish" lifestyle by working in the Canadian film industry as a database clerk, earning him the affectionate title of "Entry Boy." He also works with police, conducting anti-homophobia workshops. His interests include writing and performing with Forte: The Toronto Men's Chorus, an organization ripe with peaches for the plucking. Chris can often be found with his tongue firmly planted in cheek—his.

GREG WHARTON is the founder/editor of suspect thoughts press and *suspect thoughts: a journal of subversive writing* (located online at www.suspectthoughts.com). His short fiction, reviews, and creative nonfiction has been widely published online and in print. He is hard at work on a collection of his short fiction and a novel.

TAMA WISE. I am a 25-year-old Maori guy from Auckland, New Zealand. I have been writing erotica for the last three or so years under the penname Anfernee Williamson. This is the first time I have published outside the Internet. My primary focus in writing is urban erotica, concentrating on stories about black, Latino and Pacific Island characters.

GREGORY WOODS is widely regarded as one of Britain's leading gay poets. His collections are *We Have the Melon* (1992), *May I Say Nothing* (1998) and *The District Commissioner's Dreams* (forthcoming, 2002), all with Carcanet Press. His critical books include *Articulate Flesh: Male Homo-eroticism and Modern Poetry* (1987) and *A History of Gay Literature: The Male Tradition* (1998), both with Yale University Press. He is professor of Gay and Lesbian Studies at the Nottingham Trent University. His was the first such appointment in Britain.

author interviews • submission information •
• resources for writers • gay literature resources
contact west beach books • links to gay litera-
previews • more about buttmen • book ex-
the author's own words • more author photos
websites • special polls • news releases • in the
books • about west beach books • in the
• advice for aspiring gay writers • links to writ-
ture resources • message boards • short stories
books • author interviews • links to gay litera-
buttmen • special previews • ebook versions •
next • more author photos • special polls •
short stories **surf's up** • submission
information • ebook ver-
sions • special features • resources for writers •
write your own review • contact west beach
about buttmen • special previews • book
in the author's own words • more author pho-
ing websites • special polls • news releases • in
books • about west beach books • in the
• advice for aspiring gay writers • links to writ-
ture resources • message boards • short stories
books • author interviews • links to gay litera-
buttmen • special previews • ebook versions •
next • more author photos • special polls •
author interviews • submission information •